SCOTTISH LEGENDS

55 Mythical Monsters

Aaron Mullins

The information provided in this book is designed to entertain the reader on the subjects discussed. Although the author has made every effort to ensure that the information in this book was correct at time of press, the author does not assume and hereby disclaims any liability to any party for any loss, damage, or disruption caused by errors or omissions. This is a unique creative writing piece, told in the author's own words, for the sole purpose of entertainment.

PRAISE FOR AARON MULLINS

"One of Scotland's best writers"
Amazon Review
★★★★★

"A master of the psychological thriller"
Amazon Review
★★★★★

"Stories that will pull you in, **fast paced with twists and turns**"
Amazon Review
★★★★★

"I really enjoyed reading this book, **very thought provoking**"
Amazon Review
★★★★★

"**Brilliant stories**, really is something for everyone in there"
Smashwords Review
★★★★★

"These short stories just pull you in from the very first page.
Brilliant stories with something for everyone to enjoy"
Amazon Review
★★★★★

"**Fascinating collection** of Scottish legends which makes the
reader wish to go on a sightseeing trip of legend locations in
Scotland. **Aaron Mullins is a compelling story-teller**"
Amazon Review
★★★★★

"**I could not put this down**, the author just pulled you in from
the very first page. Each story makes you stop and think about
life and friendships"
Amazon Review
★★★★★

"**Aaron hits top 100 list** with Highland mystery tales"
John O'Groat Journal

"It has already **featured in the Amazon top 100 bestsellers** for crime, thriller and mystery short stories, alongside books by Stephen King and Dean Koontz"
Press and Journal

"If you love **suspense with good humour** then look no further"
Amazon Review
★★★★★

"I was excited to get my hands on this book! It is packed full of short wee legends and is great to pick up and put down. **Very well written, as you would expect from an Aaron Mullins book**, and gives you just enough of a tingle down your spine!!"
Amazon Review
★★★★★

"engrossing and **entertaining collection** of short stories …would make a five-star-rating popular TV drama series **…universal storytelling at its best**"
– Review by Carol McKay (author and reader for The Highland Book Prize) of *Mysteries and Misadventures: Tales from the Highlands*
★★★★★

"His love for the Highlands and its people shines through, both in his stories and reflections on his personal journey"
Caithness Courier

"They arrive like sprites. **Whispering in his ear**, buzzing around in his mind, walking around his consciousness, forcing their way into his thoughts. The shadows at the edge, the inspiration for his next writing project"
Ayrshire Magazine (Interview with Aaron Mullins)

DEDICATION

For those who delight in the danger of adventure.
May you always overcome the monsters you meet.

"Fantasy, myth, legend, truth – all are intertwined in the
story that is Scotland."

- *Laurence Overmire*

AARON MULLINS

FICTION
Mysteries and Misadventures: Tales from the Highlands
Scottish Urban Legends: 50 Myths and True Stories
Scottish Legends: 55 Mythical Monsters
Scottish Killers: 25 True Crime Stories
Mullins Collection of Best New Fiction
Mullins Collection of Best New Horror

WRITING GUIDES
How to Write Fiction: A Creative Writing Guide for Authors

BUSINESS GUIDES
How to Write a Business Plan
The Ultimate Business Plan Template

PSYCHOLOGY
The Effect of Mate Value on Self-esteem
Social Responsibility and Community Resilience
Risk Perception in Extreme Event Decision Making
Ethnic Differences in Perceptions of Social Responsibility
and many more...

www.aaronmullins.com

CONTENTS

PREFACE

Scottish mythical monsters have always been a fascinating part of the rich history and folklore of the land. Ancient Scots were curious about the world around them and their fantastical explanations of natural phenomena often involved the creation of mythical creatures with amazing powers.

Nowadays, we might understand that a loud rumble from the sky is thunder and not some ancient angry beast. Yet more recent sightings of these legendary monsters indicate that not everything can be explained away by modern science. There's still plenty of myth and magic throughout the land, waiting for brave adventurers or careless trespassers to stumble across their secrets.

Scottish monster myths can give insights into the local customs and folklore of their time. However, they also mimic the stories brought to the shores from other cultures, in particular, monsters from Norse legends.

Early Scots not only fought against the human warriors of the Viking invaders but also against their cultural tales. Norse beasts battled against Scots legends, fighting to become the dominant fable. Inevitably, a little of the Viking heritage intertwined with Scottish history to produce the myths and legends we know today.

What makes Scottish myths somewhat unique though is that, unlike Greek, Roman, Norse and other similar well-known legends, they aren't generally concerned with the adventures of a pantheon of Gods. Instead, it's the giants, monsters and other astonishing creatures, particularly of the sea, that dominate tales of Scotland's past.

In this book, you'll meet many mythical creatures from Scottish folklore. Climb mountains to meet giants, hide in the dark from wailing apparitions and voyage beneath the waves to meet monsters that haunt the depths of the sea. Learn which beasts may still run wild through the Scottish countryside and why handsome strangers are rarely what they seem.

Like the tales told in my book *Scottish Urban Legends: 50 Myths and True Stories*, the real power of these Scottish stories lies in their ability to not only entertain us as monster tales in the present, but also to forge a living link to our past. New generations can enjoy the legends and feel connected to the land and its people.

Scotland, like its national animal, the mythical unicorn, has a proud, untameable and magical element to its landscape, stories and its people.

Let these timeless tales remind us of simpler times when the tides were the breath of a great sea dragon and thunder was the angry roar of a living god. Mythical beasts that still live on in our hearts and minds, with every re-telling of their legendary deeds.

Aaron Mullins

www.aaronmullins.com

GOBLINS AND TRICKSTERS

BLOOD AND BLESSINGS

Gruesome goblins have terrorised farms and castles across Scotland since legends began.

Some of these tricksters would play foul pranks upon lazy servants, while others indulged in deadlier pursuits. From creatures who bestowed kind blessings on weary travellers, to fiends who crept down chimneys at night to steal away small children.

This chapter explores the legends and folktales surrounding these mythical creatures. We will also examine why there exists such conflicting accounts of their true nature, both the bloody and the benign.

BAUCHAN

(Scottish: *bòcan*. English: *bauchan*, *buckawn* or *bogan*)

A bauchan is a type of Scottish hobgoblin with conflicting personality traits. At times, the bauchan can be kind and helpful, but at others it's reputed to have been a roguish and sometimes harmful creature.

Descriptions of bauchans vary greatly between legends, ranging from small, hairy creatures that were similar in appearance to brownies (another mythical creature that we will investigate later), to huge monsters more akin to giants or trolls.

We will take a look at two tales that illustrate both sides of these strange creatures. The small and sometimes helpful soul and the fearsome monster it could become.

Within the book *Popular Tales of the West Highlands* by John Francis Campbell, there lies a tale of a farm in Lochaber that was frequented by a mythical bauchan.

The owner of the farm, Callum Mor MacIntosh, developed a peculiar relationship with the bauchan that was sometimes hostile in nature but could also be friendly and constructive at times.

The bauchan would often help out with daily chores around the farm, but could also become quarrelsome and start fights with Callum. Magical in nature, the bauchan was a shapeshifter who would emphasise its stubborn nature by taking the form of a goat.

One fight between Callum and the bauchan is said to have started over a handkerchief, which had been blessed and given to Callum by his wife. The bauchan decided that the handkerchief would be suitable payment for the help he had been giving Callum around the farm. As it was a gift from his wife, Callum refused to part with it and told the bauchan that if he wished to own the handkerchief then he would have to take it from him. Which, after a strenuous struggle, the bauchan successfully did.

Later, perhaps feeling guilty about depriving Callum of his wife's gift, the bauchan returned the handkerchief. This highlights the dual nature of this mythical creature. An aspect further seen one particularly bad winter.

Callum's farm had been cut off from the surrounding area by a horrific snowstorm and he was unable to gather wood for his fire. Upon seeing the plight of his sometimes-friend, the bauchan felled a great tree so that he could provide enough firewood to Callum and his family to see them through the harsh winter storm.

Perhaps tiring of the cold Scottish winters, or the bauchan's antics, Callum and his family emigrated to New York. However, the bauchan followed them there and life is said to have continued in the same contradictory manner it always had. The bauchan helped Callum prepare his new land, but also fought him when the mood took him.

Although he couldn't escape from the bauchan by moving to America, at least Callum was fortunate that he didn't encounter the fearsome type of bauchan that appears in our next tale.

Coluinn the Headless was said to be a huge, murderous bauchan that stalked the area between Morar House and the River Morar, in the west Highlands. Travellers along this area, known as the Smooth Mile, feared being attacked and killed by the mythical beast.

However, the terrifying bauchan would only attack men. Women and children were free to roam the area without fear. In addition, he would not attack members of the family that lived at Morar House, suggesting that the creature was in fact protecting the grounds from potential threats.

Unfortunately, one day the bauchan attacked and killed the wrong traveller. The victim was a distant relative of the MacLeod clan from Inverness and a close friend of the chief's son, Iain Garbh. Upon learning of his friend's death at the hands of the vicious bauchan, Iain swore vengeance and set off to hunt the mythical beast. Stalking along the Smooth Mile, Iain found the bauchan and a great battle ensued.

Iain managed to overpower the bauchan and pinned the creature in place throughout the night until the first rays of dawn stripped Coluinn the Headless of his strength. Iain spared the defeated bauchan who promised to leave and never return to the Morar area. Coluinn is said to have lived the rest of his days secluded away on a hill in northern Skye.

In *The Haunted Wizard*, by Christopher Stasheff, a bauchan tricks the main character into naming him 'Buckeye', thus cursing him with a bond with the creature.

BODACH

(Plural: *bodaich*. Old Irish: *botach*)

A bodach is a hobgoblin-like creature, which gets its name from a Scottish Gaelic term for 'old man' and is often associated with being unlucky or evil.

In literal terms, the meaning of the name bodach can be derived from the Scottish Gaelic 'bod', meaning penis, and the suffix 'ach', which translates to 'someone who has a penis' but more generally means 'mature person'.

So how did a creature named after a mature person's penis come to be considered so evil?

For the answer, we must look to Scottish parenting techniques, where legends warn that the bodach will sneak down the chimney at night and attack or steal away naughty children. It was used as a bogeyman-type myth to scare children into behaving.

The soot-coated bodach would locate the mischievous child sleeping in their bed and pinch, pull and poke their victim until they cried out from the nightmares this attack evoked. Sometimes, if the child had been particularly naughty, they would be whisked away by the bodach to places unknown, never to be seen again.

One defence against the bodach was said to be putting salt in the hearth, as the creature would not cross the salt and therefore be unable to emerge from the bottom of the chimney.

The bodach has a reputation of being unlucky due to its association with being an omen of death. In the novel *Waverley*, by Sir Walter Scott, Fergus MacIvor meets a 'Bodach Glas', a creature that foretells his coming demise.

The *Odd Thomas* series of books by American author Dean Koontz describe bodachs as bad omens who appear at locations of impending disasters to feast upon the destruction and misery. In the series, Odd had the ability to see bodachs, which would gather around people who were about to die, or would cause the deaths of others.

One day, while working as a cook at a California diner, Odd meets a customer who is being followed by a large number of bodachs. This suggests that the man is about to be involved in a large scale disaster with enough pain to feed an entire swarm of bodachs.

Koontz has taken the legend of the bodach as an omen of death and put his own twist on it to transform a myth into a modern story.

Other authors have simply taken the hobgoblin-like aspects of the bodach and used them to populate their worlds, like the spear-wielding creatures seen in *The Moon of Gomrath* by Alan Garner.

In modern times, the bodach forms part of a tradition surrounding a family of stones in a secluded part of Scotland. Hidden inside a wild shelter near Meall Daill, Perthshire, is a set of stone carvings said to be the Cailleach (a mythical female deity who can control the weather), the bodach (her husband) and their children.

Their exact location is a closely guarded secret, in order to preserve the ancient stone carvings. Known as both Tigh Nan Cailleach (house of the old woman, after the Cailleach) and Tigh Nam Bodach (house of the old man, after the bodach), accessing their hiding spot is no easy feat.

A determined explorer would have to hike across 8km of demanding and treacherous terrain, including boggy marshland north of Loch Lyon.

Scottish myths say that the Cailleach, the bodach and their children were offered shelter during a terrible snowstorm. Thankful for the kindness shown to them, the Cailleach carved their likeness into the stones and blessed them with her powers. Legend tells that as long as the family of stones is shown the same care and shelter that the real family was shown, then the glen will always be fertile.

To this day, those who are tasked with the preservation of the stones bring them outside every year to mark Beltane (around the start of May) and bring them in again every Samhain (last day of October).

This means the family of stones gets to enjoy the summer months outside but are given shelter every year for the winter months.

Given the bodach's bogeyman-nature and evil portent of doom reputation (and being married to a divine hag who commands the storms), it's probably best that this tradition to care for his family continues for many more centuries to come.

BROWNIE

(Scots: *broonie*. Scottish Gaelic: *brùnaidh* or *gruagach*)

A brownie is similar to a bodach, but said to be more reclusive in nature, preferring to emerge at night to do chores around the home. In return, the owners should leave out a food offering for the brownie by the fireplace, usually a small bowl of milk or cream.

This relationship the brownie builds with their chosen household can last for entire lifetimes. However, should the family take advantage of the helpful creature, or offend it in some way, then the brownie will leave the home and never return.

Servants who live in the household must also pull their weight during the day, as the brownie has been known to play pranks on anyone it believes is being lazy and leaving all the work for the mythical creature. They can even turn violent if they feel extremely insulted by the behaviour of the humans with whom it shares its home.

Human-sized in older tales, modern brown-skinned brownies are often described as being short, ugly and hairy, but also very wise. They are very comfortable being naked or dressed only in the barest of rags and will leave a household if the owner attempts to clothe them. Some tales tell of their ability to shape-shift, taking on the form of various animals, particularly when attached to a farmhouse. They can also turn invisible, which helps them with the mischievous pranks they pull on any slothful servants.

The name brownie has been adopted as a universal description of these creatures across the UK, but they are sometimes known locally by other names throughout Scotland, England and Wales, such as hobs, ùruisgs and Bwbachs. It's the brownie name though that has become commonplace in literature and culture.

The Girl Guides have a younger age group called Brownies (of which my daughter is a member) who are named after a short story called *The Brownies*, in the book *The Brownies and Other Tales* by Juliana Horatia Ewing.

The short story is based on the mythological culture of the brownies and contains a small, lazy boy who does not want to do his chores. Feeling sorry for himself, the boy calls out for a brownie to complete them for him. However, a wise owl takes pity on the boy and informs him that brownies are a myth and that the real brownies of the world are simply good and helpful children who complete their chores. Inspired by the owl's wisdom, the boy rushes home and tells his brother what he has learned. Together, they decide to become the 'brownies' of their household, doing as many chores as they can.

The popularity of Ewing's book led to good, helpful children being called brownies as a positive compliment. This in turn inspired the Girl Guides to adopt the name for their younger members, who complete helpful tasks to earn badges. Initially called Rosebuds, Lord Baden Powell's sister Agnes (a co-founder of the Girl Guides/Girl Scouts movement) suggested the name 'Brownies', who were helpful little creatures from a story she loved.

Solitary creatures, brownies usually work alone and are said to live in caves, streams, rocks or other natural homes near the households that they serve. Occasionally, the family may even learn the name of their brownie, such as Meg Mullach (also known as Hairy Meg), who was one of the few female brownies. Regional variances in descriptions also exist, with brownies from Aberdeenshire said to have no fingers or toes, while brownies from the Scottish Lowlands had a hole where their nose should be.

A minister of the Church of Scotland, John Brand, wrote a book about his travels around Orkney and Shetland (circa 1701) spectacularly entitled *A Brief Description of Orkney, Zetland, Pightland-Firth & Caithness, Wherein, After a short Journal of the Author's Voyage thither, These Northern Places are first more Generally Described.*

In his book, Brand states that forty or fifty years prior to his visit to the islands, nearly every family had a brownie in their household. They were commonly known to the islanders as being evil spirits that should be appeased with a sacrifice of milk. Many households even had a rock called a 'brownie's stane', which had a small hole to hold offerings of wort (a grain extract).

A brownie legend from Peeblesshire warns of the consequences of meddling with these offerings. According to the tale, some bannock (Scottish scone-like bread) and a bowl of milk left out for the brownie were stolen by two of the household maids. When the two thieves sat down to eat their meal, the brownie turned invisible and secretly placed himself between them.

Every time one of the maids attempted to drink the milk or eat the bannock, the brownie stole it from them. This led to the two thieves arguing and accusing each other of further theft, until the brownie revealed himself and laughed at the foolish pair.

These pranks were reserved for the other servants of the household. Should the owners have committed such an act, then the consequences may have been more serious. If suitably angered, brownies are said to have gone on violent rampages, destroying all the work they had helped with.

In extreme cases, the brownie may even turn into a 'boggart', which is essentially a similar creature in folklore tales, but with greater evil intent. Not least because boggarts can shape-shift into the form of a person's greatest fear.

This was demonstrated in *Harry Potter and the Prisoner of Azkaban*, by J. K. Rowling, when Professor Lupin is teaching the class the boggart-banishing spell Riddikulus, turning their fears into something humorous.

Apart from stealing their offerings, one of the quickest ways to anger a brownie was to criticise their work. A legend from Cranshaws in Berwickshire tells of a brownie that had worked hard all day mowing and thrashing the grain, a task it had excelled in for several years. However, the brownie was insulted when somebody commented that the grain had not been mown or stacked correctly. Under the cover of darkness, the disgruntled brownie stole the grain, carried it for two miles and threw it off the cliff at Raven Crag. As he did so, the brownie sang:

'It's no' weel mow'd! It's no' weel mow'd!
Then it's ne'er be mow'd by me again;
I'll scatter it owre the Raven Stane
And they'll hae some wark ere it's mow'd again!'

It's not always direct criticism that lands a person in trouble though. Sometimes, even the simplest of things can anger a brownie, such as giving them a nickname.

A Perthshire legend tells of a brownie who lived in Almor Burn, near Pitlochry, who enjoyed nothing more than splashing about in the water and then walking up to the nearby farmhouse each night. Being an extremely fickle creature, if he found everything in the house a mess, he would tidy it for the family. But if he found everything was already tidy, then he would make it messy again, much to the disdain of the owner and servants who lived there.

This continued until one evening when a man was walking by himself along the path near the burn. He heard the splashing of water and called out to the brownie who he knew resided there. Not knowing the brownie's true name, the man called him 'Puddlefoot', to which the splashing immediately halted, the brownie gasped in shock and cried out 'I've gotten a name! 'Tis Puddlefoot they call me!', before disappearing from the burn forever.

Tales of even smaller slights show just how fickle these creatures could be. A brownie from Bodsbeck, near Moffat, became offended enough to leave after a farmer had the gall to call out to let him know his cream had been poured, rather than let the brownie discover this for himself.

One of the most popular elements of brownie legends is that giving the creature an item of clothing will result in the brownie leaving the household.

This legend was drawn upon in *Harry Potter and the Chamber of Secrets*, by J. K. Rowling, when Harry Potter tricks Lucius Malfoy into gifting his house-elf, Dobby, with a sock. This means that Dobby is now free to leave the Malfoy family.

Traditional brownie legends suggest that, rather than being thought of as a gift, brownies are insulted by the gesture. This is supported in *The Discoverie of Witchcraft*, by Reginald Scot, who noted that brownies would often chant angry rhymes before they departed. Examples of this from Scottish brownies are:

Gie Brownie a coat, gie Brownie a sark,
Ye'se get nae mair o' Brownie's wark.

Red breeks and a ruffled sark!
Ye'll no get me to do your wark!

Other explanations suggest that these mythical creatures are actually being punished or cursed and the act of giving them clothing frees them, allowing them to return to Fairyland (or a similar place where brownies reside).

One brownie tale that lends support to the curse theory is the Cauld Lad of Hylton, named such (cauld is a Scottish variant for cold) because he could often be heard at night muttering rhymes that lamented his predicament.

Thinking they were helping him, the servants of the household gave the cold creature a green mantle, causing him to sing loudly with joy at the gift:

Here's a cloak, and here's a hood!
The Cauld Lad of Hilton will do no more good!

Then, like the others, he disappeared forever.

Perhaps brownies were bound by a set of rules of which we were unaware, cursed to serve a human family until they are presented with the gift of clothing. Mistreating or insulting the brownie may also have set them free, within the terms of their servitude. Though it would seem that this type of punishment or curse is no longer in use in brownie culture.

This culture is similar to that of other mythical creatures, such as elves and fairies, but very much unique. Brownies live solitary lives, rather than the groups in which fairies are often encountered. They often reside in man-made dwellings, rather than living in the wild. In *Minstrelsy of the Scottish Border*, by Sir Walter Scott, he states that brownies are 'a class of beings distinct in habit and disposition from the freakish and mischievous elves'.

But why did such a distinction arise between brownies and other mythical creatures of their kind?

Myths and legends often teach us valuable wisdom or serve a purpose as a cautionary tale. So why were these rarely seen creatures said to be so helpful, yet so fickle?

For the answer, we need to look at our own cultural history and why the belief in brownies was rather useful for everybody in the household. Folklorists believe that, in pre-industrial times, brownies were a fabulous tool with which homeowners could keep their servants in line.

A belief in brownies would ensure that servants didn't grow lazy, lest they become a victim of the mischievous creature's pranks. Therefore, brownies were a fine example for owners of being hardworking and rarely seen, commendable traits they wanted to see in their servants at that time.

However, this belief worked both ways. For if the homeowner also believed in brownies, then servants could blame their mishaps on a mythical creature that came during the night and bumped around, made a mess or broke household items. Servants could also suggest that extra food, milk and cream be left out, which they could then consume each evening. This made the legend of brownies a mutually beneficial belief.

Perhaps they are no longer seen today, as modern households have more earthly victims to place the blame of mischievous acts on, should one not leave out a nightly sacrifice of a bowl of milk and some food by the fire. These fickle, purring creatures, described as being short and hairy, have helpfully slaved away protecting the house from various rodents all day. But if you try to give them the gift of clothing, they will likely become insulted, turn violent and disappear for an extended period of time. Are cats the brownies of modern society?

One Scottish poet and novelist who had been charmed by the myth of the brownie was James Hogg. In his novel, *The Brownie of Bodsbeck*, food items are mysteriously being stolen from a farmhouse. The ending comes with a twist though, as the 'brownie' was in fact famous Covenanters leader John Brown, hiding out nearby.

In his short story, *The Brownie of Black Haggs*, Hogg draws upon the supernatural aspects of brownie culture to ensure an evil woman gets what she deserves. Lady Wheelhope arranges the murder of any servants who openly practice religion. Men are shot and women are poisoned until she comes head to head with an ugly servant called Merodach, who is short like a young boy but has the wrinkled complexion of a hundred-year-old man. Merodach's religion is an ancient one with pagan origins, greatly offending Lady Wheelhope. Although never openly called a brownie, Merodach fits the description and refuses to be paid for his services. He also manages to avoid all attempts on his life. Instead, Lady Wheelhope's plots and schemes mysteriously go awry, accidentally leading to the deaths of people close to her.

As time passed, these violent stories gave way to a more child-friendly version of brownies that began to dominate popular culture. From Thimbletack in *The Spiderwick Chronicles* to Big Ears in Enid Blyton's *Noddy* series, brownies were now cute, fantastical creatures. They served as mascots for the Cleveland Browns American football team and the St. Louis Browns baseball team. This demonstrates the enduring nature of this mythical creature, whose intriguing tales have forever shaped many aspects of modern life.

DUNNIE

A dunnie is a distant relative of the brownies who resides along the Scottish border near Roxburghshire, Berwickshire and Northumberland.

Smaller than a brownie, a dunnie is said to have the same brown-coloured skin and ugly, hobgoblin-like appearance. Unlike its house-dwelling cousins though, dunnies are far more likely to live in the mountainous areas along the Scottish borders.

In particular, they were often encountered by those who travelled through the craggy cliffs and valleys of The Cheviot Hills, on the northern edge of Northumberland National Park.

You could tell when a dunnie was nearby as they would sing their famous song:

In Cockenheugh there's gear eneugh,
In Collierheugh there's mair,
But I've lost the keys o' the Bounders, (*or Bowden-door*)
I'm ruined for evermair.

Ross for rabbits, and Elwick for kail,
Of a' the' towns e'er I saw Howick for ale:

Howick for ale, and Kyloe for scrubbers,
Of a' the towns e'er I saw Lowick for robbers;

Lowick for robbers, Buckton for breed,
Of a' the towns e'er I saw Holy Island for need;

Holy Island for need, and Grindon for kye,
Of a' the towns e'er I saw Doddington for rye:

Doddington for rye, Bowisdon for rigs,
Of a' the towns e'er I saw Barmoor for whigs:

Barmour for whigs, Tweedmouth for doors,
Of a' the towns e'er I saw Ancroft for whores:

Ancroft for whores, and Spittal for fishers,
Of a' the towns e'er I saw Berrington for dishes.

This song was noted by Michael Aislabie Denham, in his work *Folk-lore: or, A collection of local rhymes, proverbs, sayings, prophecies, slogans, &c. relating to Northumberland, Newcastle-on-Tyne, and Berwick-on-Tweed.*

Between 1846 and 1859, Denham published 54 various pamphlets and other works relating to folklore tales he had been told. These publications came to be collectively known as the Denham Tracts. Highly influential, they are rumoured to be where J. R. R. Tolkien first discovered the word 'hobbit', nestled innocently amongst a list of known fairies.

The most famous of all the dunnies is the Hazlerigg Dunnie, who is said to be the restless spirit of a 'reiver'. Reivers was the collective name for a group of both Scottish and English raiders along the Anglo-Scottish border, operating from the late 13th century to the beginning of the 17th century.

While alive (and still very much human) the Hazlerigg Dunnie is said to have claimed several victims and was struggling to carry all his ill-gotten loot, so he stashed it within a hidden rocky cavern.

His treasure concealed, the reiver continued his raids on the nearby village of Hazlerigg. Unfortunately, while robbing corn from the granary, he was discovered by the locals and a violent struggle ensued.

Eventually, the farmers overwhelmed the thief and put him to death. Before he died, he vowed that he would not rest because it took too many people to take him down and his treasure was still stashed away in the nearby hills.

It's said that his ghost, the Hazlerigg Dunnie, still haunts the area, where he enjoys frightening children and playing pranks on unsuspecting victims. One of his favourite tricks is to shape-shift into the form of a plough-horse and wait until the local farmer has fitted a harness, walked him to the stables and completed all his horse-care chores, before disappearing and laughing at the shocked farmer's response to the harness suddenly falling to the stable floor.

Other times, he would allow the rider to climb upon his back and trot along pleasantly, before vanishing and landing the rider in the muddiest part of the road.

He would also facilitate the exchange of babies between the human and fairy realms by disguising himself as the horse that the midwife arrives on.

It's unknown whether his stashed loot was ever recovered.

MAGGY MOULACH

(Other Names: *Meg Mullach*, *Maggie Moloch*, *Maug Moulack*, *Maug Moulach*, *Mieg Moulach*, *Maug Vuluchd*, *May Moulach*, *Meg Molloch*, *Manch Monlach* and *Hairy Meg*)

Maggy Moulach is perhaps the most famous (or infamous) of all the brownie-like mythical creatures from the Scottish Highlands. Being a typical brownie, she was brown-skinned, short (around 2 foot tall) and rather hairy, leading to her unfortunate nickname of Hairy Meg.

Maggy lived with her son, Brownie-Clod, in Tullochgorm Castle and served the owners, the Grant family, through the usual chores carried out by a brownie. Maggy's additional duties included acting as a banshee, to announce the deaths of family members, and teaching chess strategies to the Grant Clan Chief so that he may defeat his opponents.

Legends say that Maggy was able to shape-shift into a grasshopper and the darker myths suggest that she was capable of coming down chimneys to kidnap children, similar to a bodach. This suggests that she perhaps underwent a transformation from good to evil.

Maggy's son was said to be a 'dobie', which is a form of brownie who has good intentions but is considered to be not very smart. He was said to guard Fincastle Mill and struck fear into the hearts of trespassers. However, one legend tells how he was tricked one night and brutally murdered by a local girl.

Maggy loved her son very much and perhaps the mixed nature of her legend is a nod to the pain she went through as she transformed from a loving mother into a vengeful spirit.

That fatal night, a girl decided to venture up to Fincastle Mill, as she desperately needed more flour to finish a wedding cake she was baking. She was aware that Brownie-Clod guarded the mill. She also knew that the miller had left for the evening and she would have to enter the mill and secretly grind the flour she needed.

Before she began grinding the flour, she put a large pot of water over a fire to boil. Unfortunately, although she tried to be extremely quiet, she had already caught the attention of the inquisitive Brownie-Clod, who burst in on her as she worked.

Wary of the bold girl who stood across from him, the dull-witted dobie spoke slowly as he demanded to know the girl's name, to which she quickly replied 'I'm mise mi fein' (I am me myself).

Undeterred, once more Brownie-Clod demanded to know the girl's name. Again she stood her ground and replied 'mi fein' (me myself). They then stood staring at each other from across the room, having reached an impasse.

Irritated by the girl's response, Brownie-Clod moved across the room towards the girl. As he stepped forwards, the girl grabbed the boiling water and launched it into his face, completely drenching the poor dobie in its scalding contents.

Brownie-Clod cried out in agony and rushed to find his mother, Maggy Moulach, who cradled her burnt son in her arms, tears rolling down her cheeks as she asked who had hurt him.

Brownie-Clod's weak reply was 'mi fein' (me myself) as he died in his mother's arms from his wounds, leading Maggy to believe that her son had somehow fatally scalded himself. The girl had succeeded in doing something that few others had rarely achieved; she had tricked not one, but two brownies.

However, the girl who defeated Brownie-Clod had become overly emboldened by her actions and bragged to all who would hear how she had fought and conquered the fearsome dobie. She imagined herself a hero of the town, freeing the mill of its terrible guardian. None seemed to question why she had gone up to the mill at that hour in the first place.

Then one day, this bravado led to Maggy hearing of the girl's actions as she walked past her window, boasting about the bravery of her deed. Some say Maggy instantly flew into a fit of rage so great that she transformed into a fearsome boggart and brought everybody's worse fears to life. Others say it was the months of heartache and grief that eventually changed Maggy.

What they all agree on is that Maggy grabbed a stool and threw it through the open window with all the strength she could muster, striking the boastful girl and killing her instantly.

To those witnessing the act, the legend of a vengeful spirit was born. The terrible Maggy Moulach, the fearsome Hairy Meg, come to wreak havoc on innocent townsfolk, killing indiscriminately and without remorse.

This was how the pain of a grieving mother became both a folklore tale and a life lesson to remain humble at all times, for the consequences of pride can be deadly.

This legend also serves as a sad story of how real-world monsters can be created by the experiences they go through. A thoroughly human lesson handed down through generations as a folklore tale.

Prior to her son's death, Maggy was known to be a jovial prankster.

One legend tells of Maggy's time spent in service to a farming household. Maggy was so efficient and hardworking that the owner of the farm fired all the other servants.

The greedy owner thought he could exploit Maggy's good nature to save himself some coin. However, it's never a good idea to take advantage of a brownie.

Maggy quickly grew tired of doing all the work and decided to not only go on strike but also play many pranks on the owner, until he was forced to rehire all the previous staff.

Another life lesson then from the legendary exploits of the mythical Maggy Moulach. Don't take people for granted.

REDCAP

(Also known as: *powrie, redcomb, bloody cap*)

A redcap is an evil goblin-like creature who makes its home amidst the ruined castles along the border between Scotland and England.

Like the other hobgoblin-esque creatures of its kind, the redcap is described as being short, strong and ugly, with the haggard skin and features of an old man. Its teeth were said to be huge and pointed, with its thin fingers sporting sharp, hooked claws, like those of an eagle. Its bright red eyes shined with malevolence from within a crop of long, straggly hair that hung past its shoulders. Atop its head, it wore its distinctive red cap.

Also commonly known as a powrie, particularly in fantasy fiction, the murderous redcap gets its name from its habit of dipping its cap in the blood of its victims. Usually armed with a pike, the redcap took great pleasure in the act of killing unwary travellers who roamed too far from home.

Those who sought shelter within the ruinous abode of the redcap quickly found themselves besieged by large rocks aimed at their heads. Should they fall, their blood would further deepen the hue of the creature's cap.

Dressed in iron boots and far stronger than any human, the only defence against the redcap was for a quick-witted traveller to wield a crucifix or utter the words of Scripture, in hopes that they would drive off the creature.

These symbols of Christianity were said to force the mythical monster to flee, or even suddenly burst into flames. Amongst the redcap's ashes could often be found a single large tooth, which was said to bring luck to anyone who carried it with them.

A similar mythical creature exists in Dutch folklore, where the Kabouter (or Kaboutermannekins) had a very different, mellower temperament and lived their lives in a similar manner to brownies, rather than the evil, castle-dwelling redcaps.

Even within Scottish folklore, there are some reports of more peaceful redcaps. One such story tells of a redcap living in Perthshire. The creature, described as being a short, placid old man, had taken up residence in a room atop Grandtully Castle, roughly three miles northeast of Aberfeldy.

Legend tells that all who met him would receive a blessing of good fortune. Perhaps he had grown tired of his kin's murderous ways along the border and decided to head north to calmer shores.

Or perhaps people who saw and heard him were confused by his choice of clothing, with his red cap possibly belonging to other mythical creatures who dressed in similar attire.

There are so many similarities between the smaller mythical creatures in legends from around the world, that it may have been difficult in times past to distinguish your bauchans from your bodachs.

In Cornwall, particular types of fairies were sometimes called 'redcaps' due to them wearing green outfits with red hats. This description is supported in a poem by William Allingham, called *The Fairies*, which contains the lines:

Wee folk, good folk,
Trooping all together,
Green jacket, red cap,
And white owl's feather!

Perhaps one of Allingham's fairies, a creature known for greater benevolence than the traditional redcap, had taken up residence in Grandtully Castle. For the other famous tales of the cruel Scottish redcaps are much bloodier in nature.

As referenced earlier, *Minstrelsy of the Scottish Border* is a collection of Scottish ballads compiled, edited and commented upon by Sir Walter Scott. Within this collection there lies a bloody ballad entitled *Lord Soulis*, by John Leyden, which tells the story of a redcap who resides in a chest that has been secured with three strong padlocks.

The redcap, known as Robin Redcap, had granted his master, Lord William de Soulis, magical protection against specific weapons used by his enemies. However, while protecting his master, the redcap had also caused huge distress and general destruction around the lands of Hermitage Castle.

According to legend, the people of the land grew tired of the redcap's antics and decided to gather together to take their frustration out on Lord Soulis.

Rather than directly use a weapon against him, the townsfolk took the doomed Lord to a stone circle near the castle called Ninestane Rig. There they wrapped Lord Soulis in lead and boiled him alive inside the makeshift cocoon.

Historically, in contrast to this mythical legend, we know that Lord William de Soulis in fact died as a prisoner in Dumbarton Castle. This was after his arrest, trial and confession for his part in the conspiracy against Robert the Bruce.

Sir Walter Scott noted that nearly every ruined castle in the south of Scotland is said to be haunted by a redcap spirit, but the infamous Robin Redcap must not be mistaken for the mischievous (but less deadly) Robin Roundcap that dwelled south of the border.

One final description of the nature of the Scottish redcap can be found in the legends surrounding the ruins of Blackett Tower, a border fortress located in Dumfriesshire.

The tower was owned by the Bell family and was said to be haunted by a redcap spirit known as 'Old Red Cap' or 'Bloody Bell'. This folklore tale supports the descriptions given by Sir Walter Scott of the redcap being a form of spirit that simply portrayed a hobgoblin-like visage.

In the poem *Fair Helen*, by William Scott Irving, the tower was said to be haunted by a murderous ghost (described as a ghastly phantom) who held a bloody dagger beneath a red eastern moon. Bringing us once again to the evil, castle ruin dwelling creatures of earlier legends.

WIRRY-COW

(Also known as: *worricow, worriecow, wurricow, wirriekow* and *wirricow*)

A wirry-cow is not a specific mythical creature, but instead an omen or symbol of bad luck, or evil, that brought great fear and distress to those who 'worried' about them.

The wirry-cow could take the form of something as simple as a scarecrow, or as grand as the Devil himself. It could be a ghost, ghoul or goblin that lingered nearby. Or even a demon, bugbear or fearsome monster.

The only thing that wirry-cows have in common is that they cause terror. In fact, a wirry-cow could even be bovine in nature, should one feel enough distress at the presence or suspicious behaviour of a common cow.

A popular word amongst many famous Scottish poets, the words 'worricow' and 'worriecows' were also used in the novel *Guy Mannering*, by Sir Walter Scott when he writes '*Wha was to hae keepit awa the worriecows, I trow? Ay, and the elves and gyre-carlings frae the bonnie bairn, grace be wi' it?*' and '*Hear ye that, ye worricow?*'.

The word itself is thought to have been coined by a Scottish minister, John Jamieson, who combined the phrase 'to worry' (meaning to harass or cause distress) with the word 'cowe', whose earlier meaning described a hobgoblin or object to be feared. The words wirry-hen, wirry-boggle and wirry-carle also describe feared villains and other ill omens.

GIANTS AND MOUNTAIN MONSTERS

TITANS OF TERROR

𝓒 olossal criminals stalk the Scottish mountain paths, striking fear into the hearts of all they meet.

These huge monsters have terrorised travellers for many centuries. Some seek revenge; others yearn for gold, or the simple pleasure of killing. Most were cut down to size, but a few disappeared without a trace.

This chapter gathers the goliaths of Scottish myths and examines how their evil deeds became folklore legends.

AM FEAR LIATH MÒR

(Also known as: *Ferlas Mor* or *The Big Grey Man*)

Am Fear Liath Mòr is the Gaelic name for The Big Grey Man, a terrifying presence said to stalk Ben Macdui, the highest mountain in the Cairngorms National Park. I became fascinated with this creature while writing my book *Scottish Urban Legends: 50 Myths and True Stories*.

This huge, dark presence brings a sense of dread as he follows hikers down from the summit of the second-highest mountain in Scotland. Which is a long and chilling experience to endure for those who have felt, or even glimpsed, the grey man just a step behind them.

Those who have laid eyes on their pursuer describe a tall creature around 10 feet in height, with a powerful build. Long, muscled arms hang from broad shoulders on his hairy body, similar to the legendary Big Foot (Sasquatch).

The Big Grey Man makes his intentions clear to any who encounter him: get off the mountain! He storms towards his victims waving his great arms angrily in a shooing motion. The dread that accompanies his presence is enough to make even the bravest hikers cry out in fear and quickly flee the area.

This feeling of terror emanates from the creature, causing hikers to panic, and is often accompanied by the horrific sounds of something heavy creeping behind them. Its footsteps have been known to follow hikers for nearly their entire descent back down the mountain.

Is this sense of dread an evil magical power that the creature employs to guard its territory?

If you feel brave enough to go in search of the creature, then you should start your hunt around the area of Ben Macdui known as Lairig Ghru Pass. This is where many hikers report they first feel the presence. Some have even stated that they have been struck by the sudden urge to leap over the cliff edge at Lurcher's Crag.

Those that do make it to safety are left with the lingering feeling that they have had a lucky escape and should never return to the mountain.

Reports of the Big Grey Man chasing trespassers out of his territory date back centuries. However, it wasn't until 1891 that his presence was taken seriously when a respected professor and experienced mountaineer encountered the mythical creature for himself.

Professor Norman Collie's trek up the mountain had gone extremely well and he reached the summit of Ben Macdui without incident. But that was where his nightmare ordeal began.

Another 34 years would pass before his tale would truly come to light when he eventually told it to a captivated audience in Aberdeen at the 27th Annual General Meeting of the Cairngorm Club in 1925.

Collie was so prolific in pioneering mountain pathways that both *Mount Collie* in Canada and *Sgurr Thormaid* (Norman's Peak) on the Isle of Skye are named after him.

Collie was also a Fellow of the Royal Society, a respected professor of Organic Chemistry at University College London and the man responsible for the first-ever medical X-ray photograph. A successful man of science who was ready to risk ridicule by telling the world that he had met a mythical monster.

Professor Collie described walking back down the mountain in a thick mist when he noticed that his footsteps weren't the only ones descending the mountain. Every few steps, his own stride was matched by the crunch of an unseen presence, slowly following behind him.

Believing that it was just a coincidence or his imagination, he took a few more steps, then waited and listened. The crunch came again, louder this time as if the unknown follower was catching up. In his own words, he described his terrifying descent:

"I was returning from the cairn on the summit in a mist when I began to think I heard something else than merely the noise of my own footsteps. For every few steps I took, I heard a crunch, and then another crunch as if someone was walking after me but taking steps three or four times the length of my own. I said to myself 'This is all nonsense'. I listened and heard it again, but could see nothing in the mist. As I walked on and the eerie crunch, crunch, sounded behind me, I was seized with terror and took to my heels, staggering blindly among the boulders for four or five miles nearly down to Rothiemurchus Forest. Whatever you make of it, I do not know, but there is something very queer about the top of Ben Macdui and I will not go back there again by myself I know."

Professor Collie's experience and vow never to return to the summit by himself contains many similarities to other encounters with the Big Grey Man. Many stories emerged as fellow mountaineers felt safer voicing their own experiences with the mythical monster, now that an esteemed climber had been the first to tell his tale.

In 1939, Alastair Borthwick published a popular book about mountaineering in Scotland, entitled *Always a Little Further*, in which he reveals the true account of two climbers who had encountered the Big Grey Man.

In the first account, a man was hiking by himself in the snow and, like Professor Collie's experience, had just begun his descent from the summit when he realised he was no longer alone. When Borthwick interviewed the man, he was told:

"I felt a queer crinkly feeling in the back of my neck," he told me, "but I said to myself, 'This is silly, there must be a reason for it.' So I stopped, and the footsteps stopped, and I sat down and tried to reason it out. I could see nothing. There was a moon about somewhere, but the mist was fairly thick. The only thing I could make of it was that when my boots broke through the snow-crust they made some sort of echo. But then every step should have echoed, and not just this regular one-in-three. I was scared stiff. I got up, and walked on, trying hard not to look behind me. I got down all right - the footsteps stopped a thousand feet above the Larig - and I didn't run. But if anything had so much as said 'Boo!' behind me, I'd have been down to Corrour like a streak of lightning!"

In the second account, a man was again hiking alone, but this time during the summer and in daylight, when a strange mist suddenly coated the mountain:

"The footsteps he heard were made by something or someone trudging up the fine screes which decorate the upper parts of the mountain, a thing not extraordinary in itself, though the steps were only a few yards behind him, but exceedingly odd when the mist suddenly cleared and he could see no living thing on the mountain, at that point devoid of cover of any kind."

Intrigued by his tale, which was so similar to other accounts, Borthwick questioned the man further:

"Did the steps follow yours exactly?" I asked him. "No," he said. "That was the funny thing. They didn't. They were regular all right, but the queer thing was that they seemed to come once for every two and a half steps I took." He thought it queerer still when I told him the other man's story. You see, he was long-legged and six feet tall, and the first man was only five-feet-seven."

The man finished his tale with a final warning:

"Once I was out with a search party on MacDhui, and on the way down after an unsuccessful day, I asked some of the gamekeepers and stalkers who were with us what they thought of it all. They worked on MacDhui, so they should know. Had they seen Ferlas Mor? Did he exist, or was it just a silly story? They looked at me for a few seconds, and then one said: "We do not talk about that."

In 1943, Alexander Tewnion was descending the mountain via the Coire Etchachan path, when he noticed he was being approached at speed by a large shadowlike form.

The hulking form brought with it a sense of danger so overwhelming that Alexander grabbed his pistol and fired three shots at the shape, before escaping towards Glen Derry. He believes he wounded whatever was following him that day.

Like most urban legends, science has attempted to explain these mysterious sightings. Their best suggestion, proposed by Johann Silberschlag in 1780, is a phenomenon called Brocken Spectre (also called Brocken Bow or Mountain Spectre), which is caused by the human eye being tricked by an optical illusion into thinking that a huge shadowlike shape is facing them.

In reality, it's actually the sun distorting their own shadow across a misty or cloudy area, which has been misinterpreted by the human eye and mind. This phenomenon has also been shown to take place from the inside of aircraft flying in the same conditions.

However, this is of little comfort to those wishing to climb Ben Macdui, because whether it is created by the human mind (or really is a mythical creature) the sense of terror that the Big Grey Man brings is still the same. An ever-present risk for those who have safely conquered the summit, but must now face the dangers that lurk in the quickly approaching mist.

BERTRAM DE SHOTTS

Bertram de Shotts (sometimes Bartram) is a mythical giant who attacked and robbed people travelling on the road between Edinburgh and Glasgow.

In the 15th century, the land around what is now Shotts village in North Lanarkshire was little more than moorland in which the giant stalked his victims.

Scottish tradesmen would transport their goods along the 'Great Road' running through the area and many valuable wares were lost to the giant's attacks.

The sheer volume of treasure that he stole (and the complaints of influential merchants) attracted the attention of King James IV of Scotland, who ordered the giant to be hunted down and killed.

Many believe that Bertram was only seven or eight feet tall, but at the time this would have been much taller than the general population, giving birth to the giant legend.

Eventually, Bertram's exploits caught up with him and he was cornered by a young hunter called Willielmo de Muirhead (or William Muirhead), the first Laird of Muirhead.

Muirhead had tracked Bertram across the moorland, following the signs and tales of the giant's violent passing. He decided to set a trap by leaving a pile of peat next to St. Catherine's Well (or St. Kate's Well) in Sallysburgh (now Salsburgh) where Bertram was known to have previously stopped to rest. Other legends say it was a large cart of heather, which Muirhead lay beneath for hours on end. Either way, he ensured he was well hidden.

Muirhead watched and waited. One day, he spotted Bertram resting to have a drink from the well. Muirhead quickly ambushed the giant, slicing both his hamstrings so that Bertram could no longer stand to fight. Showing no mercy, Muirhead then decapitated Bertram, ending the giant's reign of terror.

Muirhead proudly transported Bertram's head to King James IV and claimed his reward, which made him a very wealthy man and saw him granted a 'Hawk's Flight' worth of land. Muirhead used this land to build Muirhead's Lauchope estate.

Despite the terror he brought to the area, there are still reminders of the legend of Bertram de Shotts along the central belt of Scotland.

Law's Castle (not to be confused with Law Castle, in West Kilbride) is a small conical hill, with several large stones scattered across the rocky knoll. Believed to be a favourite hideout of Bertram, these stones and the moorland bowl around them are known as the Giant's Cup and Saucer.

The village of Shotts, located roughly midway between Edinburgh and Glasgow, is also thought to have been named after the mythical giant. His story was recorded in Sir Walter Scott's *Minstrelsy of the Borders*, as well as in a 1922 Scots poem by Robert Dangster.

BIASD BHEULACH

(Also known as: *Biasd Bealach, Beast of Odal Pass*)

The Biasd Bheulach was a shapeshifter who roamed the Odal Pass on the Isle of Skye, from Kylerhea (Caol Reatha) to the Sound of Skye.

Sometimes taking human form, but generally appearing as an animal, the creature is also known as Biasd Bealach Odail – the Beast of Odal Pass.

This nocturnal mountain monster was described in the 1902 book *Witchcraft and Second Sight in the Highlands and Islands of Scotland*, by John Gregorson Campbell.

In it he writes:

"Sometimes it bore the form of a man, sometimes of a man with only one leg. At other times it appeared like a greyhound or beast prowling about, and sometimes it was heard uttering frightful shrieks and outcries which made the workmen leave their bothies in horror. It was only during the night it was seen or heard."

The monster began terrorising workmen when the first public road was being made through the Odal Pass, keeping them awake at night with horrific screams.

Those who travelled through the pass reported being attacked by a man, or a one-legged man, or even a large greyhound, all of which are attributed to the shape-shifting ability of the Biasd Bheulach.

The most famous of its victims was a man who was found dead at the side of the road with mysterious injuries. He lay with one hand over his leg and the other on his side, both palms covering the wounds that had killed him.

In his book, Campbell writes:

"It was considered impossible that these wounds could have been inflicted by human agency."

Adding to the mystery, all attacks by the Biasd Bheulach stopped after the body had been found. One final victim with unexplainable injuries.

But why did the attacks suddenly cease?

In her 1976 book, *An Encyclopedia of Fairies*, folklorist Katharine Briggs suggests that the mythical beast may have been the ghost of a murdered man seeking revenge. Once it had attacked those responsible, it moved on.

However, the attacks appear to have been random, including against people simply passing through the area, undermining this theory of focused revenge attacks.

It could be that the creature still roams the area, but travellers no longer stop there overnight, so he hasn't had anybody within his territory for a long time.

Or perhaps the attacks ceased because the final victim himself, with his strange injuries, was in fact the shapeshifter. Maybe somebody had figured out an ancient ritual to finally stop the Beast of Odal Pass.

FACHAN

(Also known as: *fachin, fachen, Direach Ghlinn Eitidh, Dithreach* or *Dwarf of Glen Etive*)

The fachan is a giant with a single eye in the middle of its face, similar to the mythical Cyclops from Greek legends. However, the fachan was described in the book *Popular Tales of the West Highlands*, by John Francis Campbell, as having some distinctly peculiar features.

Instead of legs, the fachan is said to have a single leg, which merges with the rest of its body. Instead of arms, it has a single hand protruding from the centre of its chest.

Upon its head grows a single tuft of hair, which may well have been a horn. As Campbell writes "it were easier to take a mountain from the root than to bend that tuft."

Not a Scottish Cyclops then, but perhaps something more akin to the Arabic legends of Nesnas or Shikk, which Campbell describes as (quite literally) half-human and able to move about with great agility on only one leg.

This description is similar to the Irish mythological creature known as the Fomor, from a race of deformed giants that the Irish gods banished to the sea.

In his book on Irish folklore, called *Beside the Fire*, Douglas Hyde suggests that these common aspects between the Scottish and Irish creatures indicate that the fachan came to be named from the Gaelic heritage of the Irish fatach (giant) and the Scottish famhair (giant).

Fachans were said to be extremely violent and hated all other creatures, both real and mythical. This was how a wary traveller could spot they had entered a fachan's territory, for no other animal could be seen or heard. The fachan had killed or driven them all away.

Fachans were also very strong and had been said to destroy entire farms. But if you could survive the initial fright of laying eyes upon the creature, then you may be able to outrun it.

Sometimes the fachan would carry a club or flail in its hand. Hyde refers to one such weapon as "a very thick iron flail-club in his skinny hand, and twenty chains out of it, and fifty apples on each chain of them, and a venomous spell on each great apple of them."

His book continues to refer to an Irish manuscript describing a mythical creature that may have been a fachan as having "a girdle of the skins of deer and roebuck around the thing that was his body, and one eye in the forehead of his black-faced countenance, and one bare, hard, very hairy hand coming out of his chest, and one veiny, thick-soled leg supporting him and a close, firm, dark blue mantle of twisted hard-thick feathers, protecting his body, and surely he was more like unto devil than to man."

There have been numerous reported sightings of fachans, but no proof of the creature's existence has ever been confirmed. For now, it remains a mythical monster, which given its propensity for hatred, violence and murder, is probably for the best.

GHOSTS AND GHOULS

APPARITIONS OF ALBA

Banshees and bogles haunt the hills and glens of the Scottish countryside. Terrifying shrieks ring out across lonely moors and gunshots pierce the darkness as moss-covered creatures are hunted by angry landowners.

Blood-thirsty vampires stalk the forests at night, luring men to their deaths, while vengeful poltergeists cause chaos in Scottish homes.

This chapter summons an army of undead creatures and explores the role they played in service to the Scottish clans, as well as learning a few life lessons along the way.

BAOBHAN SITH

The baobhan sith is a female vampire who seduces her victims by appearing as a beautiful woman, only to turn into a violent creature of the night.

Haunting the Scottish Highlands, the baobhan sith is a popular figure in works of fantasy. The *Dancing Vampire* series, by Cornelia Amiri, portrays the adventures and love lives of seven baobhan sith sisters.

In the Scottish urban fantasy series *Caledonia*, by Amy Hoff, a baobhan sith leads the Fae army. The trilogies *The Age of Misrule*, *The Dark Age*, and *Kingdom of the Serpent*, by Mark Chadbourn, regularly feature the baobhan sith. On the big screen, *Baobhan Sith* was released in 2017 by a Scottish film company.

One dark night in the Highlands I even fought a baobhan sith myself, as a child armed only with a pencil and some dice, in my much-treasured *Vault of the Vampire* book from the *Fighting Fantasy* series, by Steve Jackson and Ian Livingstone.

Scottish folklorist Donald Alexander Mackenzie states in his book *Scottish Folk-Lore and Folk Life* that the vampiric baobhan sith appear as beautiful women, in order to seduce men, who they then completely drain of blood. Often draped in a long green dress that conceals the deer-like hooves they have for feet, the baobhan sith has the ability to transform into a hooded crow or raven. But like most vampires, they must return to their lairs with the rising of the sun.

Mackenzie goes on to tell the tale of four hunters being attacked by the baobhan sith while out in the wilderness late at night.

After a successful day's hunting, the men decided to camp for the night in an isolated and roughly constructed shieling (a hillside hut normally used to shelter shepherds and their animals, similar to a bothy).

To relax, the men decided to dance and sing, with one of them saying to the others how great it would be if they also had some female partners to dance with.

Not long after that declaration, four beautiful women mysteriously appeared at the hut.

One of the women sat by the singer, while the other three partnered up with the dancing men. The voice of the singer faltered as he noticed drops of blood falling from his fellow hunters.

Terrified, the singer fled from the hut and hid amongst the horses. The mysterious woman who had been seated beside him chased him into the night but was unable to find him. The hunter survived to see the first rays of dawn and returned to the hut to discover the other men were dead, their bodies having been completely drained of blood.

In her book *An Encyclopedia of Fairies*, Katharine Briggs also refers to this famous baobhan sith legend, suggesting that the hunter unknowingly saved his life by hiding next to the iron hooves of the horses, as iron was a known vulnerability of these creatures.

In an alternative version of this legend, one of the hunters notices that the women have hooves instead of feet, causing him to flee. He returns later to discover the other men dead with their throats cut and chests ripped open.

A third version of this legend tells that the hunters had actually made camp in a cave. Feeling lonely, each of the men wished that their partners were there with them, except for one man, Macphee, who said he preferred his wife to remain at home as he had his dog for company.

Shortly after, a group of beautiful women entered the cave and murdered the men who had wished for their partners. Macphee was the sole survivor, protected by his loyal dog who drove the vampires from the cave.

It would seem that the baobhan sith are attracted to those who speak their desire for female company.

This is in line with traditional Scottish beliefs that you shouldn't make a wish at night without also invoking God's protection.

This is because creatures of the night are always listening, waiting for an invitation to enter your life and grant your wish, but in an unexpected and sometimes deadly manner.

So should you one day find yourself sheltering in a bothy on a Scottish mountain, relaxing after a hard day's hunting, you should be very careful what you wish for.

As you might just get it.

CAOINEAG

(Also known as: *caointeag, caoineachag, caointeachag* and *caoidheag*. Similar to: *caointeach*)

The caoineag (pronounced khoo-nyak) is a Highland banshee who would foretell the death of Scottish clan members by crying during the night, normally at a nearby natural feature, such as a loch or waterfall. With her name derived from the Gaelic caoin (meaning weep) and caoidh (meaning mourn), this sombre 'weeper' spirit is almost always invisible. The caoineag is classified as being one of the Fuath (meaning 'hatred' in Gaelic) a group of malevolent Highland spirits that frequent Scotland's waters.

Unlike the bean nighe (another legendary Scottish banshee that we'll meet in a later chapter) the caoineag was an immovable omen of death that couldn't be approached, questioned or made to grant wishes. Every clan had their own caoineag and if you heard her cries you would ask *Co tha siad?* (Who is that?). The response you would receive is *Co ach Caoineachag, co ach Caoineachag bheag a bhroin* (Who but Caoineag, who but little Caoineag of the sorrow).

Carmina Gadelica is a compendium of hymns, charms, incantations, blessings and many other forms of folklore from the Gaelic-speaking areas of Scotland. The works were gathered together by folklorist Alexander Carmichael in the late 19th century and the caoineag features within the six-volume collection. Carmichael writes that the legendary banshee would always foretell the death of clan members slain in battle, causing great anxiety to families whose sons were about to march to war. It is said that the caoineag of the MacDonald clan wept and wailed loudly for many nights prior to the Massacre of Glencoe in 1692, where an estimated 30 members of the clan were murdered by Scottish government forces for (allegedly) not pledging allegiance to the new monarchs, William III and Mary II.

Carmichael states that the caoineag even sang mournful dirges prior to the massacre, recording her lament as:

Little caoineachag of the sorrow,
Is pouring the tears of her eyes,
Weeping and wailing the fate of Clan Donald,
Alas my grief that ye did not heed her cries.

There is gloom and grief in the mount of mist,
There is weeping and calling in the mount of mist,
There is death and danger, there is maul and murder,
There is blood spilling in the mount of mist.

Some members of the MacDonald clan had been so terrified by the caoineag's weeping that they fled the glen before the government forces arrived, thus escaping the grisly fate suffered by the clan members who stayed.

Another caoineag legend is remembered through the folktales of the MacKay clan from the Rinns of Islay. When death was stalking an unwell member of the MacKay clan, their caoineag would stand outside the door of the sick person's house and shriek her banshee wail. This let the family know to make peace with their loved one, as the end was inevitable.

However, one night the caoineag was shrieking outside the windward door of a MacKay family member when something peculiar occurred. A member of the sick person's family felt such sorrow for the mournful spirit that he went outside the leeward door and placed a plaid on the ground, before slipping quietly back inside.

He then called out to the caoineag: 'Come to the sheltered side of the house, poor woman, and cover yourself with a piece of my plaid.' Suddenly the banshee's weeping stopped. The family waited, but she was not heard from further that night or in the Rinns ever again.

The caoineag is often linked to a similar (alternative) death spirit called a caointeach. They are so closely associated that, in his Scottish Gaelic dictionary, Edward Dwelly even suggests caointeach as an alternative spelling of caoineag, which he defines as a 'female fairy or water-kelpie'.

Like the caoineag, each clan in Islay is said to have had its own caointeach. With similar banshee duties, but dressed in a green shawl, rather than being invisible, the caointeach would linger outside the door of a sick person's home and weep.

In a very similar tale to that of the MacKay caoineag, one legend tells that a caointeach was accidentally caused to be banished from the premises when she was presented with a gift of clothing from the family. This aspect of the caointeach folktale resembles the behaviour of the household brownies seen at the beginning of this book. In all likelihood, the caoineag and the caointeach are probably two names for the same mythical Scottish spirit of death.

BOGLE

(Also known as: *boggle, bogill, shellycoat, barghest, brag, hedley kow, ettin, yetun, yotun, etene, yttin* or *ytene*)

As you can tell from the variety of alternative names, a bogle is a broad term for a number of similar creatures, all of whom take great pleasure in setting cunning puzzles, rather than working for (or killing) the humans they meet.

The origins of the name bogle are thought to stem from the German word bögge, from which the word 'goblin' is also derived (böggel-mann). This German word also influenced the Middle-English term 'bugge', from which the term 'bogey' (and thereby bogeyman) is also derived.

There may have been further global influences, in either direction, from the Norwegian word 'bugge' (meaning 'important man') and the Welsh 'bwg' (also bwga, or bwgan, meaning ghost, or hobgoblin). The term 'bagairt', which means 'threat' in Irish Gaelic, may also have been an influence.

Many names then, for what is in essence the same legendary creature that came to be known as the bogle.

Returning to a more Scottish influence (particularly where I live in Ayrshire) one of the most famous mentions of the mythical creature was by the National Bard himself, Scottish poet and lyricist, Robert Burns (familiarly known as Rabbie Burns). At the beginning of Tam O' Shanter, Burns quotes Scottish bishop and fellow poet Gawin Douglas: 'Of Brownyis and of Bogillis full is this Buke.'

One famous Scottish legend tells of the exploits of Tattie Bogle, who was often described as looking like a scarecrow. The cheeky creature loved hiding in potato fields and jumping out on unsuspecting humans, sometimes even causing potato blight in his hiding spot.

It has been suggested, though, that the 'Tattie Bogle' legend, with its scarecrow-like description, may actually have been a cunning ploy by Scots farmers to keep the children out of the potato fields.

A Scots poem by W. D. Cocker, called *The Bogle*, also describes the many annoying and scary antics associated with this mythical creature.

Outside of Scotland, the antics of bogles have been front-page news. On the 31st March 1866, the *Larne Weekly Reporter* ran a sensational story entitled *Bogles in Ballygowan*.

The article told the story of a particular house in rural County Antrim, Northern Ireland, that was reportedly under attack from bogles. Stones and other missiles were raining down upon the property from unseen sources, breaking windows and even penetrating the roof.

Everybody in the area was terrified, but just as suddenly as the attacks began, they mysteriously ended.

It was concluded that the sustained ordeal was a revenge attack by bogles who had taken offence at the recent refurbishments, which used material from an older property known to be frequented by the 'little people'.

GLAISTIG

(Also known as: *maighdean uaine* or *green maiden*)

The glaistig is a Scottish ghost who (like both the baobhan sith and the caointeach) often appears as a beautiful woman in a green dress with a grey visage and long yellow hair. However, her attire is simply a disguise for the lower half of her body, which resembles that of a goat.

The strangest thing about the glaistig is her ambivalent nature, sometimes acting kindly, at other times becoming evil. A fickle faun-like ghost then, who can be both mild and monstrous, depending on her mood.

Similar to the baobhan sith, some legends tell of the glaistig luring menfolk to her lair with seductive dances, where she then kills them and drains them of all their blood. The evil version of the glaistig would also try to divert travellers from their path through force, with the throwing of heavy stones a favourite trick.

In contrast, the kinder glaistig is portrayed as a protector of cattle. One Scottish legend from the town of Ach-na-Creige tells of a glaistig who would help protect the cattle and herders, in return for some milk. She's also said to have helped watch the children while their fathers drove the cattle and their mothers milked the cows. The villagers would pour the milk into a hollowed-out stone, similar to the offerings given to the bauchans. However, one day a young scoundrel poured boiling milk into the stone, burning the kind glaistig. She immediately stopped her helpful ways and left the farm shortly after.

Another tale from *Superstitions of the Highlands and Islands of Scotland*, by John Gregorson Campbell, suggests that glaistig legends originate from the time a human noblewoman was granted (or cursed with) a 'fairy' nature, leading to her goat-like legs and ghostly immortality, wearing her green dress for all eternity.

In some glaistig tales, this apparition is said to protect the home and take care of those weak of mind. But in others the glaistig was murdered in her green dress and hidden in a chimney by a servant, only to return as a vengeful spirit.

There are several 'Green Lady' legends from around Scotland, including the Green Lady of Crathes Castle that I wrote about in my book *Scottish Urban Legends: 50 Myths and True Stories*, who may have been a murder victim. The discovery of grisly human remains inside a fireplace where she regularly appears supports this theory. Scottish Green Lady spirits can also be found roaming the halls of Fyvie Castle, Ashintully Castle, Ballindalloch Castle, Knock Castle and a host of other places around the country.

In popular literature, the glaistig appears in the story *Waycross* by Caitlín R. Kiernan, as a dark faery queen literally called *The Glaistig*. The urban fantasy novel *War for the Oaks*, by Emma Bull, and the young adult series *Wicked Lovely*, by Melissa Marr, also both contain mythical glaistigs.

It would seem that the dual nature of the glaistig legends arise from how the spirit was treated. Treat her kindly and you'll receive kindness. A lesson then in her tales.

SILKIES

Silkies are female spirits who wore rustling silk gowns and inhabited the border between Scotland and England. They were quiet, solitary ghosts who made no sound, other than the swishing of their silk dress as they worked.

Silkie is often used as an alternative spelling of 'selkie', which is another mythical creature (capable of switching between human and seal form) that we will look at in a later chapter. Silkies also shouldn't be confused with the breed of chicken bearing the same name!

Due to their name's association with their water-based cousins, information on silkies is notoriously difficult to find. Though they are listed in *The Encyclopedia of Ghosts and Spirits* by Rosemary Ellen Guiley.

Legends say that silkies would often act like bauchans, helping around the farm and household and guarding families against those who wished them harm. This included killing intruders, showing their dangerous side.

Also, like bauchans, silkies could be mischievous and play pranks on other servants and family members or even leave households in a mess. If angered, they would throw possessions and break furniture. Being a spirit, this led to them being thought of as poltergeists.

There was a time when Scottish law prohibited those of the working classes (below aristocracy) from wearing silk. So completing her chores in a silk gown made the silkie all the more extraordinary.

GHILLIE DHU

(Also known as: *Gille Dubh*)

The Ghillie Dhu is a male fairy with dark hair who lives alone in the birch forests of Gairloch in Wester Ross, a village in the North-West Highlands.

Scottish lexicographer, Edward Dwelly, states that his name translates from Scottish Gaelic as dark-haired lad. It's derived from the English word ghillie (a variant of the Scottish Gaelic word gillie), meaning a lad, youth or boy, combined with dubh, which means dark or dark-haired.

Generally, the Ghillie Dhu is a shy creature dressed in an outfit of moss and leaves, to blend in with its forest home. He chooses to avoid contact with adult humans until they stray too far from the path and invade the glades and groves of his territory. He will then become aggressive towards these trespassers and attempt to drive them away.

However, the Ghillie Dhu is also known to be kind and gentle towards children, helping them find their way back to the path if they become lost.

Legend tells that in the late 18th century a young girl from a nearby village, Jessie Macrae, became lost in the woods. Jessie had stumbled far from the path and darkness had fallen. The Ghillie Dhu found the poor girl tired, hungry and very afraid. Seeing her distress, he made her a small shelter and comforted her during the night, keeping her protected and warm, before leading her through his forest and safely home the following morning.

In the aftermath of Jessie's emotional return home, the local landowner, Sir Hector Mackenzie of Gairloch, decided the Ghillie Dhu was to blame for her being missing all night. He gathered a group of Mackenzie dignitaries who attempted to hunt and capture the creature. The team of five men set off with guns one evening and hunted through the night, but could not find the creature anywhere. After the failed hunt, it is said that the Ghillie Dhu was never seen again.

The book *Strange and Secret Peoples,* by Carole G. Silver, refers to an expert on congenital disorders, Susan Schoon Eberly, who suggests the Ghillie Dhu wasn't a fairy or nature spirit at all but was instead a human being with a medical condition. The small stature of the creature suggests a form of dwarfism, with an outfit gathered from his surroundings after making his home in the woods. This would explain why he avoided the adults of the time, who were less understanding of his condition, but was kind to children. After being hunted, he may have decided to move to safety within quieter woods. It may also explain why he was sighted within the time period of an adult human life span but then disappeared. In all that time, Jessie was the only person that he ever spoke to.

Regardless whether he was a spirit or a human, all the Ghillie Dhu wanted was to be left alone to live in peace.

The ghillie suit, an item of camouflage clothing that allows the wearer to blend into forest foliage through the use of twigs and leaves (often worn by snipers on military operations), gets its name from this Scottish legendary creature.

BIG CATS AND WILD BEASTS

WOLVES AND WILD THINGS

Werewolves and wild beasts roam the Scottish hills and forests. Their terrifying howls keep locals awake at night and the remains of their victims are found when daylight returns.

Some beasts attain such legendary status that they are discussed in the House of Commons, while others are potentially proven to be an accidental hoax.

This chapter explores a menagerie of mythical cats, dogs, pumas, wolves and spectral animals that haunt the land, and how their legends have influenced Scottish history.

BEAST OF BUCHAN

The Beast of Buchan is a big cat that has been sighted mainly in the Buchan area of Aberdeenshire since the 1930s. Given the number of sightings over a long period of time, some say that the beast is actually a phantom cat.

Around the middle of the 18th century, exotic pets were likely being transported across Scotland to new homes on large estates, or even performing with travelling circuses. In 1868, the *Empire* newspaper (based in Sydney, Australia) reported about a leopard hunt in Scotland, after five of the big cats escaped from their cages while being transported between Lockerbie and Moffat.

Fortunately, all the leopards were recaptured, but how many other incidents went unreported around this time?

Could an escaped beast have survived and possibly bred with native cats, leading to sightings for nearly 100 years?

Big cat sightings from around the time of the Second World War have been attributed to pumas owned by the United States Army Air Forces. If the pilots who owned the creatures did not return from a mission, then their puma mascots were set free in the Scottish countryside.

In 1976, the Dangerous Wild Animals Act came into law to deal with the increasing fashion of people in the late-1960s and early-1970s keeping wild animals as pets. Around this time it's believed that many large cats were released into the wild by owners who were unable to meet the licensing conditions laid out in this new legislation.

In 2006, *The Guardian* newspaper reported that there may be as many as 7,000 sightings per year of big cats roaming around the UK. The *Sunday Herald* newspaper revealed that the Beast of Buchan had been reported 22 times to Grampian Police between May 2000 and January 2002, but the majority of sightings likely aren't reported.

Scotland on Sunday reported that, between 2000 and 2006, there were 50 sightings reported of the Beast of Buchan, ranging from Ardersier (a small fishing village in the Highlands) down to Fraserburgh, Inverurie and even near the English border.

The majority of sightings though have been in and around Aberdeenshire. So prevalent was the beast that in 1997 Alex Salmond (who was the leader of the Scottish National Party (SNP) at the time) raised the issue of livestock attacks on Scottish farms in the House of Commons.

In 2002, the beast even attacked a human. A woman was pounced upon when leaving a stable near Insch and the beast bit and clawed at her leg, before being chased away. Her friend witnessed that attack, describing a black, cat-like animal the size of a Labrador which had left bruising and puncture marks on her friend's thigh.

That same year, Richard Lochhead (SNP Member of Parliament for northeast Scotland) requested a formal enquiry regarding attacks by the beast. This was carried out by Ross Finnie, who was at that time Minister for the Environment and Rural Development. The threat of attack from the Beast of Buchan was being taken very seriously.

Livestock attacks took place again in 2006 when *The Press and Journal* reported that a farmer from Cruden Bay had discovered one of his sheep torn apart, following sightings by his workers of a huge cat prowling the area. In 2008, *The Scotsman* told the tale of a woman who had spotted the beast again and in 2011, a large, black beast was spotted twice by a man from Old Deer.

Hunts for the elusive beast have not been successful, leading some to whisper that the creature is in fact a phantom cat. The Cù Sìth is a Scottish mythological hound, as large as a small cow, with shaggy, dark green coats. The Cat-Sith (which we look at later) is its feline counterpart, possibly inspired by sightings of Kellas cats, a hybrid of domestic and wildcats.

In 2009, *The Press and Journal* reported that the Beast of Buchan had been captured alive in a chicken shed. The creature had also attacked a German Shepherd, but after examination by a wildlife veterinary surgeon, it was deemed to simply be a large wildcat and was set free.

A mounted specimen of a Kellas can be seen at The Zoology Museum at the University of Aberdeen, but these cats are generally considered too small to kill a fully grown sheep. The woman attacked in 2002 also knew what Kellas cats were and was adamant she was attacked by a much larger creature. That same year, *The Press and Journal* reported the discovery of a headless carcass belonging to a larger than average feline, which was too big to be a Kellas.

But until the day we successfully capture the creature, the Beast of Buchan remains a mysterious legend.

BEITHIR

The beithir is a huge serpent which appears at night when lightning strikes. The name beithir is a Scottish Gaelic word that various sources attribute with different meanings, including serpent, lightning and thunderbolt.

The large snake-like creature is sometimes called beithir-nimh (venomous serpent) and nathair (serpent or adder). In his *Dictionary of Celtic Mythology*, James MacKillop states that its name may also mean 'wild beast' and originate from the Norse word for 'bear'.

In 1908, folklorist E. C. Watson wrote in the *Celtic Review* that the beithir was a venomous and destructive creature. She suggested that the destructive nature of lightning and the devastation it left behind were the basis for the beithir legends.

In *Popular Tales of the West Highlands*, John Francis Campbell suggests it was a wingless dragon-like serpent. But in *Superstitions of the Highlands and Islands of Scotland*, John Gregorson Campbell describes the beithir as the largest and most deadly kind of serpent.

Campbell states: 'The big beast of Scanlastle in Islay was one of this kind. It devoured seven horses on its way to Loch-in-daal. A ship was lying at anchor in the loch at the time, and a line of barrels filled with deadly spikes, and with pieces of flesh laid upon them, was placed from the shore to the ship. Tempted by the flesh, the 'loathly worm' made its way out on the barrels and was killed by the spikes and cannon.'

Legend says the beithir lives in a mountain cave and hunts with its venomous sting. If a person is unfortunate enough to be stung by the serpent, they must race towards the nearest river or loch. If they can touch the water before the beithir, then they will be cured. But should the beithir reach the water first, they will succumb to its venom.

A different legend states that the only way to cure the beithir's venom is to douse the victim in water in which the head of a normal snake has been soaked. But beware when beheading that snake, because the myth goes that if you cut off the head of a normal snake, you must put some distance between its head and body, or the parts will reconnect and return to life as a beithir.

In *Scottish Folk-Lore and Folk Life*, Donald Alexander Mackenzie suggests that the beithir may be a new form of the mythological hag known as the Cailleach Bheur. Legend says the Cailleach was trapped and killed by a hunter who chopped her body into pieces. However, he didn't move the parts far enough from each other, so she magically reformed as a serpent-dragon.

Another tale, retold by John Francis Campbell, tells a fairytale-like story of a wicked stepmother who happened to be married to an Irish king. One day the evil stepmother presented the king's son with a magic shirt, which was actually a shape-shifting beithir in disguise. As soon as the prince put the shirt on, he fell under his stepmother's enchantment. Eventually, he escaped the curse with the help of a wise woman. Perhaps during the next thunderstorm, we should all look a little closer to see what the lightning reveals.

BLACK DOG

American folklorist, Stith Thompson, created the six-volume *Motif-Index of Folk Literature* which is a catalogue of folklore motifs (granular elements of folklore) commonly known as Thompson's motif-index.

Within this index, the black dog motif is recognised as an aspect of folklore that is present in many different forms and origins. The black dog is frequently a demon, ghost or shapeshifter that comes out at night and is possibly the Devil in disguise or one of its minions.

A night-time appearance of a black dog apparition, which is half the size of a horse and has large glowing eyes, is thought to be an omen of death. Alby Stone's *Infernal Watchdogs, Soul Hunters and Corpse Eaters* traces the mythical origins of these legendary beasts and finds they often appear at places associated with death, such as crossroads and ancient pathways, where many executions were carried out.

Black dogs are also sometimes associated with electrical storms, but the origins of these popular legends come from many sources. Throughout history, European legends have associated black dogs with death or being evil hounds of the Devil. The Greek Cerberus, the Norse Garmr and the Welsh Cŵn Annwn are all guardians of the Underworld.

Alby Stone suggests that this may be due to them being scavengers by nature that will even eat corpses. Some legends have the dogs directly attack humans, while others merely have them appearing as sinister warnings.

The legend of the black dog as a portent of death can be seen in the Harry Potter series by J. K. Rowling, where the 'Grim' is described by Harry's divination teacher Professor Trelawney as being a 'giant, spectral dog that haunts churchyards' and is the worst omen of death. Harry then goes on to believe he meets the Grim in person in *Harry Potter and the Prisoner of Azkaban*, but it turns out that it was Sirius Black, an animagus who has the ability to turn into a large black dog.

A few legends have the black dog act benevolently and others indicate they may be guardians who guide travellers at night, helping them stay on the right path and guarding them against danger. This was certainly how the black dog that Harry Potter met acted, secretly guarding him and giving him a frightening nudge in the right direction onto The Knight Bus.

Led Zeppelin's song *Black Dog* references a stray dog that would wander around the recording studios, but also draws on elements of the black dog legends. Possibly the most famous of all the ghostly black dogs can be found in *The Hound of the Baskervilles* by Sir Arthur Conan Doyle, where the creatures symbolise death. One of the mythical creatures terrorises a family estate and the fabled detective Sherlock Holmes is hired to unearth whether the hound is a real creature or a ghostly apparition.

Finally, in Scottish myths, black dogs are also guardians of treasure. There's a standing stone close to the village of Murthly, near Perth, where legend says that anybody brave enough to move the stone will discover a treasure chest guarded by a black dog.

CAT-SÌTH

(Also known as: *Caith Sidhe* or *Cat Sí*. Plural: *Cait-Shith*)

The cat-sìth is a large, spectral black cat with a white spot on its chest that haunts the Scottish Highlands. Some legends say the cat is a fairy-like creature, while others suggest that it's actually a witch who has the ability to transform into a cat nine times.

The origins of the cat-sìth legends may have come from the hybrid Kellas cats, which are only found in Scotland. Being all black, save for one white spot, it's easy to see how similar legends (such as the Beast of Buchan) can spring up from tales of these large cats.

Descriptions of cat-sìths often refer to them as having their backs arched and bristles erect, which is what an unwary traveller would find, should they happen to startle a Kellas cat in its natural habitat.

The famous British folktale *The King o' the Cats*, which was featured in *More English Fairy Tales* by Joseph Jacobs in 1894, tells the story of a man who had encountered the mysterious cat-sìth.

In the tale, a woman is sitting by a fire one winter evening with her large, black cat Old Tom. Meanwhile, the woman's husband is walking down the street when he sees nine black cats with white spots on their chests carrying a coffin with a crown on it. As the procession passes him, one of the cats turns to the man and asks him to 'Tell Tom Tildrum that Tim Toldrum is dead."

The man rushes home to his wife and tells her what he saw. Suddenly, their cat leaps up and exclaims 'What?! Old Tim dead! Then I'm the King o' the Cats!' before he shoots up the chimney and is never seen again.

According to Scottish legends, the cat-sìth were not to be trusted as they would attempt to steal your soul by passing over your corpse before you are buried. This belief led to vigils called the Fèill Fhadalach (Late Wake) being held, where bodies were guarded around the clock to keep the cat-sìth away. Should a cat come near the body during this time, it would be distracted with games, riddles, music, wrestling and catnip. No fires were lit near the corpse, as the cat-sìth might be attracted to its warmth.

During the Gaelic festival of Samhain, legend says that any household that left a saucer of milk out for the cat-sìth would be blessed and those who didn't would be cursed. This is similar to the trick or treat tradition of Halloween, whose festivities fall on the same night as Samhain.

One particularly gruesome ritual apparently involved summoning a demonic cat-sìth called Big Ears, who would grant any wish to those who summoned him but required the burning of the bodies of cats for four days and nights.

As previously mentioned, a popular belief was that the cat-sìth were actually witches who could transform into cats nine times. However, on the ninth transformation, the witch would be stuck in her cat form forever. Some believe this may have been the origin of the common notion that cats have nine lives.

CÙ-SITH

(Also known as: *Cú sídhe*. Plural: *Coin-sith*)

The Cù-sith (which means fairy dog) are legendary spectral hounds that roam the rocky hillsides of the Scottish Highlands. Often described as being the size of a small cow, the cù-sith can be recognised by their distinctive shaggy, dark green coats. This is in line with other fairy realm creatures who traditionally wear green.

Legend says that the cù-sith would bark loudly three times, a blood-curdling sound that was heard by everyone for miles around. If you heard it, you would have to reach a place of safety by the third bark or die of fright, with your heart stopped by the terrifying yowl. When men heard the cù-sith's bark, they would lock away any women who were nursing babies. This was so that the cù-sith couldn't kidnap them and whisk them away to the fairy realm, where they would be forced to feed the children of the daoine sìth (fairies believed to be the forefathers of the gods and goddesses of nature).

The cù-sith was usually a silent hunter, despite having paws the size of a man's hand. If you met the mythical hound, its fiery, glowing eyes and long curling tail would strike fear into your heart. And worse, you would be in danger, as the cù-sith is believed to be a harbinger of death who would appear to lead the soul to the afterlife, the fairy realm, or the underworld (depending on which legend you believe). The clefts of rocks in which the cù-sith made their home were also thought to be fairy mounds, to aid their travel between the realms.

GALLOWAY PUMA

The Galloway Puma is believed to be a phantom cat that stalks the forests of Dumfries and Galloway.

In the late 1990s, *The Independent* newspaper reported that Canadian tourists had spotted the cougar-like Galloway Puma while on a nature walk in Galloway Forest, near Kirroughtree.

In 1999, this account was supported by many residents of nearby Newton Stewart who also claimed to have seen the elusive big cat.

This was followed by a flurry of reports from local farmers and Forestry Commission employees that they had also spotted the big black cat known as the Galloway Puma. The majority of sightings were centred around the Machars area.

In June 2001, *The Galloway Gazette* reported that there was a 'Puma Sighted Near Newton Stewart'. The article detailed the terrifying experience a Newton Stewart resident had, while out walking her dog near the golf course, which borders Galloway Forest.

The lady said a 'large black cat, bigger than an alsatian' leapt out at her while she was walking along the pathway near the edge of the course. Fortunately, her dog started growling and barking at the big cat, which caused it to flee.

The woman was left startled and shaken at her encounter with the now-legendary Galloway Puma.

PICTISH BEAST

(Also known as: *Pictish Dragon* or *Pictish Elephant*)

The Pictish Beast is one of the most mysterious of legendary creatures. The name refers to an artistic drawing of an unidentified animal that regularly appears on Pictish symbol stones.

While not fully resembling any living animal, the Pictish Beast is thought to look most similar to a seahorse, particularly when viewed upright. This has led to many researchers suggesting it could be anything from a dolphin, to a kelpie, or possibly even the Loch Ness Monster.

However, modern research has indicated that the creature may be related to legendary dragons. This is due to its similarities to S-shaped dragonesque style brooches created between the mid-1st and 2nd centuries.

These artistic brooches have been discovered in southern Scotland and northern England and depict fantastical creatures, such as doubled-headed dragons with swirled snouts and distinctive ears.

Researchers believe the Mortlach 2 stone (a class I symbol stone found in 1925 during grave-digging at Mortlach churchyard) shows a strong resemblance to the shape and alignment of a brooch, depicting a Pictish Beast.

Whatever this legendary creature was, it was very important to the Picts, accounting for 40% of all Pictish animal despictions.

GIGELORUM

(Also known as: *Giol-Daoram*)

The Gigelorum is the smallest and, arguably, the strangest of legendary creatures. Tom M. Devine and Paddy Logue discuss the Gigelorum in a book published by Edinburgh University Press, entitled *Being Scottish: Personal Reflections on Scottish Identity Today*.

The researchers state that Scottish folklore legends describe the Gigelorum as being the smallest of creatures, so tiny that it is able to inhabit the ear of a mite.

If we go back in time to 1900, in his *Superstitions of the Highlands and Islands of Scotland*, John Gregorson Campbell suggests that the creature's name may have come from the smallest insect that can be seen with the naked eye. The giolcam-daobhram can only be seen by those with excellent eyesight and was described at the time as 'an animalcule, the smallest supposable living thing'.

However, others argue that the Gigelorum doesn't exist and the legend may have actually been created by the imagination of Campbell himself.

Ronald Black (a Celtic studies lecturer, author and journalist) points to the fact that no additional authoritative sources exist that further reference the mythical creature. We can conclude that either the folklorist Campbell was fantastic at storytelling, or he had indeed captured the only details in existence about the rarest of legendary creatures.

WULVER

(Similar to: *werewolf* and *weredog*)

The wulver is a kind, part-human and part-wolf creature that lives on the Shetland Islands. In the book *Myths, Gods and Fantasy: A Sourcebook,* by Pamela Allardice, the wulver is said to have been a friendly and generous creature that looked like a person covered in short, brown fur, with the head of a wolf.

The wulver would fish alongside locals and share the fish they caught, but could become angry and violent if provoked (a somewhat human trait too).

In the 1932 book *Shetland Traditional Lore,* by Jessie Saxby, she describes the mythical creature:

'The Wulver was a creature like a man with a wolf's head. He had short brown hair all over him. His home was a cave dug out of the side of a steep knowe, halfway up a hill. He didn't molest folk if folk didn't molest him. He was fond of fishing and had a small rock in the deep water which is known to this day as the "Wulver's Stane". There he would sit fishing sillaks and piltaks for hour after hour. He was reported to have frequently left a few fish on the window-sill of some poor body.'

Unlike the traditional werewolf, the wulver is not a shapeshifter and maintains its wolf-like humanoid appearance at all times. The legendary creature was never human and is unaffected by the phases of the moon.

Like most people, wulvers just want to live out their lives in peace. They will happily help lost travellers and leave fish on the windowsills of poor families.

Folklore researcher and expert in congenital disorders, Susan Schoon Eberly, believes that these human traits displayed by the wulver may be because the legendary creature actually *was* human. In her article *Fairies and the Folklore of Disability: Changelings, Hybrids and the Solitary Fairy*, Eberly suggests that the wolf-like features and fur coating its body may have been caused by a medical condition, such as Hunter syndrome.

This view angered many people and caused quite a stir within the academic folklorist community. In his 2021 article for the Shetland Museum Archives entitled *The real story behind the Shetland wulver*, Brian Smith completely dismisses the existence of the wulver. Smith goes further, stating that it was Jessie Saxby herself that started the legend when she misinterpreted one of her sources.

Smith points out that Faroese scholar Jakob Jakobsen and Shetland folklorist John Spence had both mentioned a hill called Wulver's Hool in their writings, stating that it was named after a fairy. However, Saxby wasn't aware that the word wulver was actually derived from an old Norse word for fairy (álf) and that, in Shetland, the vowel á often turns into 'wo'.

So in her writing, Saxby believed she had unearthed the 'wulver' as a unique mythical creature native to the Shetland Islands. But in reality, she may have accidentally started a legendary hoax.

GNOMES AND FAIRY FOLK

COURTS AND KINGDOMS

Dark fairies and their lighter cousins hold court over these pages. Tales of the flying host of the unforgiven dead are brought into the light.

We will hear about the origins of the mother of witches whose influence still permeates modern traditions and the true-life tales of murders committed by those believing they were killing fairy changelings.

This chapter uncovers the secrets of the 'little people' of Scottish myths and attempts to understand how their existence is used to explain a number of natural monuments throughout the land.

CHANGELING

(Also known historically as: *auf* or *oaf*)

Legends say a changeling is a fairy child that is left behind after the fairies steal away a human child. Fairies would sometimes even leave a very elderly fairy in place of the human child so that they could be cared for in their old age. The changeling initially has the exact physical appearance of the human child it replaced, but over time, as the child ages, there are said to be ways to identify a changeling.

If a child becomes sickly and doesn't grow in size at the rate expected of a healthy human child, then this may be a sign that they are a changeling. More prominent clues are said to be long teeth or even a beard. If a child is intelligent for their age, beyond expected levels of knowledge or insight, then this may also be a sign that they are a changeling. In Scottish folklore, a changeling may also be caught performing odd acts when alone, such as jumping around, dancing or playing an instrument.

With this description, I'm beginning to suspect my own daughter may in fact be a changeling! When I spoke to her about my concerns she just gave me a look that said 'don't be ridiculous' and carried on combing her beard.

To protect their children from being stolen by fairies, parents would place simple charms around their child's sleeping area. These included inverted coats and open iron scissors, as well as keeping an ever-watchful eye on the child.

In his 1997 essay *Changelings*, D. L. Ashliman provides a sombre reason for the origins of the changeling myth. Ashliman states that, in pre-industrial Europe, life was hard and many families struggled with poverty. Many peasant families relied on every member of the family being productive, as they couldn't afford to provide for somebody who was a drain on their few resources.

Sadly, this meant that if a child was born with a physical or mental disorder (which weren't understood very well in those days) then, as Ashliman states:

'The fact that the changelings' ravenous appetite is so frequently mentioned indicates that the parents of these unfortunate children saw in their continuing existence a threat to the sustenance of the entire family. Changeling tales support other historical evidence in suggesting that infanticide was frequently the solution selected.'

This suggests that changeling accusations were simply an emotional distancing and justification for the murder of children. However, legends say that fairies would also steal away fully grown adults.

The fairy folk would be particularly likely to kidnap new mothers, who were then used to nurse newborn fairies. When they stole away an adult, they would often leave an object (such as a log or rock) in their place, which had the likeness of the human, but would soon sicken and die.

Sometimes though, a friend or relative would notice a change in a person's behaviour and conclude that they were a changeling. And a few did something about it.

One of the most famous adult changeling legends (and folklore criminal cases) is the murder of Bridget Cleary.

Bridget was an Irish woman who was murdered by her husband, Michael, in 1895 because he believed that the real Bridget had been kidnapped by fairies. Michael killed the changeling to force them to return his wife, creating a national scandal.

When Bridget fell ill with bronchitis, Michael and her father accused her of being a changeling. They performed a number of gruesome rituals to cast the fairy out, including throwing urine on her, and eventually her burnt corpse was found in a shallow grave.

Nine people stood trial for the part they played in the wounding and murder of Bridget Cleary. The jury learned that Michael was attempting to force-feed Bridget by pinning her to the floor near the kitchen fire and torturing her with a burning piece of wood.

Unfortunately, Bridget's clothing caught fire. Instead of helping, Michael doused her body with the kerosene from an oil lamp and prevented others from going near the burning body, telling them that Bridget was in fact a changeling and he was attempting to get the fairies to return his real wife.

It was never established whether Bridget had already died of her torture wounds, or whether she was burnt alive. Michael Cleary was found guilty of manslaughter and sentenced to 20 years of penal servitude, of which he served 15 years.

In a 2006 article, psychiatrists H. O'Connell and P. G. Doyle suggest that Michael Cleary may have actually been suffering from a psychotic disorder. This may have been brought on by the stress he was under as he watched his wife dying of bronchitis. The helplessness he felt at saving her from a real sickness may have caused his mental health to decline, to the point where he rationalised saving her from a mythical ailment instead.

Capgras syndrome is the belief that a familiar person has been replaced with a duplicate. In this case, it quickly developed into a case of *folie à plusieurs* (a syndrome in which two or more individuals share symptoms, such as delusions). A number of songs and books, both fictional and non-fiction, reference the case. An Irish children's rhyme also contains the lines: *Are you a witch, or are you a fairy/Or are you the wife of Michael Cleary?*

Sadly, the murder of Bridget Cleary is not an isolated case. In 1826, Anne Roche bathed Michael Leahy, a four-year-old boy who was unable to stand or speak, three times in the River Flesk. On the third time, the boy drowned. Anne claimed that the boy was a changeling and she was attempting to drive the fairy out of him. Her 'fairy defence' led to her being acquitted of murder.

In Scottish folklore, those who lived along the Anglo-Scottish border believed that fairies lived in small natural mounds known as fairy hills. They would sometimes replace human children in the area with changelings, who could only be revealed by tricking or surprising the child into speech or laughter beyond its years.

In *Folklore of Northumbria*, Fran and Geoff Doel describe a legend where a mother suspected her child of being a fairy (or elf) changeling. One day a neighbour proves the mother's suspicions to be true when she runs into the house shouting 'Come here and ye'll see a sight! Yonder's the Fairy Hill a' alowe' (the Fairy Hill is on fire). To this, the elf child stood up and said 'Waes me! What'll come o' me wife and bairns?' and climbed up the chimney.

Another legend from the Scottish borders comes from the ballad of *Tam Lin*. In this tale, Tam Lin is a fairy who steals the virginity of a maiden while she walks through the forest of Carterhaugh. Upon informing her father of her pregnancy, the woman (usually called Janet) returns to the forest and Tam reappears. The pair talk and the woman learns that Tam used to be a mortal man, who fell from his horse and was captured by the Queen of the Fairies.

Tam informs Janet that every seven years the fairies give one of their people as a teind (tithe) to Hell. Tam believes he will be chosen as the sacrifice that night, which also happened to be Halloween. Janet decides to rescue Tam from this fate and together they hatch a plan.

Tam will ride past that night as part of a company of eleven knights and Janet will recognise him by his white horse. She must pull him from the horse and hold him tight. The fairies will try to make Janet drop Tam by transforming him into all manner of strange creatures, but he promises not to harm her. Eventually, he will turn into a lump of burning coal and at that point Janet must cast him into the well. He will reappear as a naked man and she must then hide him.

Janet follows these instructions and rescues Tam from the Queen of Fairies. This legend and others like it are the origins of Scottish folklore that say a human child can be offered as the tithe to Hell, which is why fairies steal them away and replace them with changelings, so that their own young may survive.

Scandinavian legends show that it wasn't just fairies that replaced human children with changelings. According to myths, Scandinavian trolls would kidnap unbaptised children and replace them with their own young. Within troll society, this was considered to be a more respectable way for their children to be raised.

A final theory about the origins of the changeling legend comes from the real-life history of communities resisting invading armies. Throughout Europe, armies would be hunting for mysterious, rarely seen people who lived in the forests and hills. Over time, the stories of these people would take on a mythical element.

It's believed that the changeling legend may have occurred due to these communities swapping their sick babies for the healthy young of the invading army, thus strengthening their own cause and hampering the occupying force.

What we can conclude is that the changeling legend was a widespread part of European society and influenced the beliefs and behaviours of people at a time when folktale explanations were more common than scientific knowledge. This created an intriguing and sometimes tragic part of human history.

NICNEVIN

(Also known as: *Nicneven* or *Nicnevan*)

In Scottish folklore, Nicnevin is a Queen of The Fairies. Her name is believed to originate from the Scottish Gaelic surname Neachneohain, which means daughter of the divine (or daughter of Scathach), or NicNaoimhein, meaning daughter of the little saint.

In Scotland and Ireland, the Celtic New Year is known as Samhain (celebrated on the same night as Halloween) and includes the Feile na Marbh (the festival of the dead). The Scottish Witch Goddess of Samhain was known by a number of names, including Nicneven. Her name was thought to have come from a Scottish woman who was accused of witchcraft and burnt at the stake in 1569.

During her trial, the woman (who was apparently over 100 years old) told her accusers that she had been accused by jealous apothecaries because her own medicines and healing techniques were far superior.

In some stories, this woman became known as the mother witch and was described by Sir Walter Scott in his *Letters on Demonology and Witchcraft* as:

'A gigantic and malignant female, the Hecate of this mythology, who rode on the storm and marshalled the rambling host of wanderers under her grim banner. This hag (in all respects the reverse of the Mab or Titania of the Celtic creed) was called Nicneven in that later system which blended the faith of the Celts and the Goths on this subject. The great Scottish poet Dunbar has made a spirited description of this Hecate riding at the head of witches and good neighbours (fairies, namely), sorceresses and elves, indifferently, upon the ghostly eve of All-Hallow Mass. In Italy, we hear of the hags arraying themselves under the orders of Diana (in her triple character of Hecate, doubtless) and Herodias, who were the joint leaders of their choir. But we return to the more simple fairy belief, as entertained by the Celts before they were conquered by the Saxons.'

Alexander Montgomerie, in his *Flyting*, also referenced the mother of witches, describing her as:

Nicnevin with her nymphes, in number anew
With charms from Caitness and Chanrie of Ross
Whose cunning consists in casting a clew.

Collections of old poems and ballads gathered by James Miller, David Laing and William Carew Hazlitt all tell various legends of the Nicnevin. In some tales, she spends her nights riding supernatural steeds with an *elrich* entourage. In others, she leaves Scotland after a love quarrel with her neighbour, to become the wife of 'Mahomyte' and queen of the *Jowis*. Her absence was said to have caused dogs to stop barking and hens to stop laying.

In Fife, the Gyre-Carling (local name for the Nicvevin legend archetype) was associated with spinning and knitting. It was said that you should never leave a piece of knitting unfinished at New Year, or the Gyre-Carling would steal it.

PECH

According to popular rhymes and fairytales, the Pech was a short and strong gnome-like race of creatures who were fond of brewing heather ale and battling against the Scots.

The Pech were described as having skin that was as tough as granite and ranged in colour from dull grey to dark brown and even a pale yellow. In *Scottish Fairy and Folk Tales*, George Douglas states that the Pech had large eyes, but lacked pupils. In *Popular Rhymes of Scotland*, Robert Chambers says their eyes reflected light like those of an owl or a cat. Both men agreed that the arms and legs of the Pech were thin and gangly, but they possessed large and powerful hands. Their hair was either a full, thick mane or wiry in nature and hung about their shoulders, the colour of wet clay.

In *The Scottish Antiquary or Northern Notes & Queries*, J. H. Stevenson says that the Pech (who were potentially related to the Picts or pixies) were believed to have worked alongside giants to build the stone megaliths scattered throughout ancient Scotland.

In one popular legend, an old blind Pech is reaching the end of his life and calls his sons to his bedside. He then asks them if he can feel their arm muscles, to see how strong they have grown. However, his sons decide to play a prank on the old Pech, placing his fingers on a strong metal cup instead of their arms. The blind Pech immediately snaps the cup with his fingers, reminding his sons that even at the end of his life, he is still stronger than them. A tale with a lesson to respect your elders.

SCOTTISH FAIRIES

Scottish folklore has been influential in classifying types of fairies, giving rise to the popular distinction of the Seelie Court and the Unseelie Court. These names are thought to originate from the Scots word *seilie* (meaning happy, lucky or blessed) and *unseely* (meaning unhappy, misfortunate or unholy). These in turn are derived from the Old English words sǽl and gesǽlig.

The Seelie Court was made up of good fairies who would help, and seek help from, humans. They would bestow favours upon those who showed them kindness, but would still turn aggressive against those who meant them harm.

The Unseelie Court was made up of malevolent fairies who would launch unprovoked attacks on humans. They often emerged at night to assault unwary travellers and were said to have aligned themselves with Scotland's evil witches.

Folklorist Katharine Briggs suggested that this light and dark categorisation of fairies may have stemmed from the medieval classification of Germanic elves of light and darkness (Ljósálfar and Dökkálfar). It's also similar to the light and dark division of Elves in Norse mythology.

In *Irish Fairy and Folk Tales*, William Butler Yeats states that there are two types of fairies. The first kind, Trooping Fairies, are good-hearted and take part in splendid processions. The second kind, Solitary Fairies, are mischievous and love to play pranks, or worse, on humans. Katharine Briggs suggests that a third category may be needed to describe fairies who reside in human households.

SLUAGH

(Scottish Gaelic: *Slúagh*. Old Irish: *Slúag*)

According to Scottish Gaelic folklore, the Sluagh or Sluagh na marbh (host of the dead) was the name given to the flying masses of unforgiven dead. The word Sluagh is believed to have been derived from the Old Irish word slúag (meaning host, army, or crowd).

In *The Magic Arts in Celtic Britain*, Lewis Spence describes the host:

'In the Western Isles of Scotland the Sluagh, or fairy host, was regarded as composed of the souls of the dead flying through the air, and the feast of the dead at Hallowe'en was likewise the festival of the fairies.'

Soaring through the skies in a crescent pattern, legends say the Sluagh would sometimes rescue humans who had become stranded on dangerous cliffs, but in general, they were more likely to grab a person and fly them far away.

In the *DeathSpeaker Codex* series by Sonya Bateman, the Sluagh don't belong to either the Seelie or Unseelie Court. Three of these independent fae characters support the main character throughout the series. In the *Merry Gentry* series of novels by Laurell K. Hamilton, the Sluagh are viewed as the lowest of the fairies, again belonging to neither the Seelie nor Unseelie Court. These dark creatures are menacing. Despite this, the main character romances the king of the Sluagh and later becomes his queen.

TROW

(Also known as: *trowe, drow* or *dtrow*)

The trow is a race of dark fairies (elves or spirits) who appear in the folklore tales of the Orkney and Shetland Islands. They are described as being short, ugly and shy, but are also very dangerous and mischievous.

The word trow may be derived from the word 'troll' of Norse mythology, or from the variant 'drow' used by Sir Walter Scott, which has a variety of meanings, including ghost, troll-folk and huldrefolk, which means the hidden people or fairies in the Shetland Norn language.

The trow emerge at night from their earthen mound dwellings (known as trowie knowes). These mythical creatures were said to break into homes while the occupants were asleep. They were particularly fond of kidnapping musicians who were then forced to play to the gathered trow.

In her book *Out Skerries - An Island Community*, Joan Dey suggests that legends of the trow may have originated from the time of Viking invasions. The shorter, dark-haired native Picts, having been forced to hide in caves, would emerge at night to attack the taller, blond-haired Viking invaders.

Trowie Glen in Hoy, on the Orkney Islands, contains geological mounds that were avoided at night, for fear of the trow living there. The Mine Howe in Tankerness, another mound, was avoided at night for the same reason.

In *The Land of the Green Man: A Journey through the Supernatural Landscapes of the British Isles*, Carolyne Larrington states that the stone circle on Fetlar was locally known as the Haltadans, which means 'Limping Dance' because legend states they were formed from the petrified bodies of dancing trow, who didn't notice that the sun was coming up and were turned to stone by the first rays of dawn.

Larrington also notes that some Shetland fiddle tunes were said to have originated from music played by the trow, that had been overheard and copied by human musicians. These are collectively known as Trowie Tunes.

In my childhood home county of Caithness, there is a mire of mounds, hollows and swamps near Canisbay, known as the Mire of Trowskerry.

In *Shetland Traditional Lore*, Jessie Saxby notes that there is a distinct race of trow known as the Kunal-Trow (King-Trow) which is comprised solely of males. Once per lifetime, these male trow take a human wife, who bears them a son, but usually dies during childbirth. This leads to the lonely males abducting a wet nurse to help feed the newborn baby. Once a powerful witch married a trow and stole all his secrets. She was able to successfully survive childbirth and brought into the world Ganfer (astral body) and Finis (an apparition who appears as a doppelganger of someone who is close to death).

The *Encyclopedia of Fairies*, by Katharine Briggs, notes that it was considered unlucky to see, hear or speak of the trow. Quietly reading about them should be fine though.

SEA SERPENTS
AND LOCH LURKERS

SOMETHING IN THE WATER

Discover which underwater creatures taught children the dangers of the sea, or acted as a warning to young maidens against meeting with handsome strangers.

Water horses run free across the surface of lochs and evil creatures attempt to kidnap humans and drag them down to the dark depths of their lair.

This chapter explores the alluring and sometimes dangerous connection between Scotland and the sea.

BEAN-NIGHE

(Also known as: *washerwoman, laundress, Les Lavandières, nigheag, nigheag na h-ath* or *nigheag bheag a bhroin*)

The bean-nighe is a female banshee known as the washerwoman due to her regularly being spotted by isolated streams and pools, washing away blood from the linen and clothing of those near to death. As a banshee, she acts as both a portent of death and, occasionally, a messenger from the Otherworld.

In *Superstitions of the Highlands and Islands of Scotland*, John Gregorson Campbell suggests that the bean-nighe is the spirit of a woman who died giving birth and is now cursed to perform these banshee activities until the day that she would have normally otherwise died. The only way to prevent this curse is for every item of the deceased woman's clothing to be washed.

If you spot the bean-nighe and slowly approach her in a respectful manner, then she may impart wisdom or grant you a wish. Though some legends tell of stranger rituals you must perform to gain access to her knowledge.

Campbell tells of a bean-nighe that frequented the Isles of Mull and Tiree who had very long breasts, which would hamper her washing of clothes, so she would sling them over her shoulders, where they hung down her back.

Should you spot this peculiar sight, you must never turn away. Instead, you should quietly approach the bean-nighe from behind and gently take hold of one of her breasts, then put it in your mouth, while claiming to be her foster child. She would then answer any questions her foster child asks her, including whose clothing she was currently washing. If she answers that it's the clothing of an enemy, you should let her continue. But if it's a friend or relative, you can interrupt her washing, thus saving the life of the otherwise doomed individual.

In *Scottish Folk-Lore and Folk Life*, Donald Mackenzie states that the bean-nighe would sometimes sing a mournful song while she worked, if a person was about to meet a particularly violent end. If you captured her, she may grant you three wishes.

Perthshire legends tell of a bean-nighe who was short, round and dressed in green, who could be caught by placing yourself between her and the stream.

Another bean-nighe who haunted the Isle of Skye was said to resemble a small child. If you spotted her first she would reveal your fate to you, but you must also truthfully answer any questions she asks. However, should this bean-nighe spot you first, then you will lose the use of all your limbs.

On the island of Islay, in the Inner Hebrides, there was said to be a Washerwoman of the Ford, who acted as a banshee and washed the clothes of those who were about to die. This version of the bean-nighe is similar to the Islay version of the Caoineag legend, another washerwoman who hated being interrupted so much that if you disturbed her, she would slap your legs with a waterlogged plaid until you lost the use of them.

Alexander Carmichael was a Scottish exciseman, folklorist, antiquarian, and author who published six volumes of Highland lore and literature, collectively called *Carmina Gadelica*, which feature all manner of folklore tales and local traditions.

The second volume in this collection features a folktale about a nigheag washerwoman, which goes as follows:

'In the dead watch of the night, 'Gille-cas-fliuch,' Wet-foot Man, of Great Clanranald of the Isles, was going home to Dun-buidhe in the upland of Benbecula— ben of the fords. And when he was westering the loch, whom should he see before him in the vista on the 'clachan,' stepping stones, but the washer woman of the ford, washing and rinsing, moaning and lamenting—

"A leineag bheag basis na dorn, A mailaran broin na beul."

Gille-cas-fliuch went gently and quietly behind 'nigheag' and seized her in his hand. "Let me go," said nigheag, "and give me the freedom of my feet, and that the breeze of reek coming from thy grizzled tawny beard is a-near putting a stop to the breath of my throat. Much more would my nose prefer, and much rather would my heart desire, the air of the fragrant incense of the mist of the mountains." "I will not allow thee away," said Gille-cas-fliuch, "'till thou promise me my three choice desires." "Let me hear them, ill man," said nigheag. "That thou wilt tell to me for whom thou art washing the shroud and crooning the dirge, that thou wilt give me my choice wife, and that thou wilt keep abundant seaweed in the creek of our townland as long as the earl of Sgeir-Iois shall continue his moaning."

"I am washing the shroud and crooning the dirge for Great Clanranald of the Isles, and he shall never again in his living life of the world go thither nor come hither across the clachan of Dun-buidhe."

Gille-cas-fliuch threw the shroud of death into the loch on the point of his spear, and he flew home hard to the bedside of Clanranald. He told everything that he saw and heard and that befell him. Clanranald leapt to his feet from the heath-bed, and he ordered a cow to be felled and a little coracle to be made ready. A cow was felled accordingly, and a little coracle was constructed, in which Clanranald went from the island over the loch to the mainland, and he never again returned to Dun-buidhe in the upland on Benbecula.'

Another Highland legend involving a banshee-like washerwoman is that of the Mermaid of Loch Slin. Alasdair Alpin MacGregor recalls this tale in *The Peat-Fire Flame: Folk-Tales and Traditions of the Highlands & Islands.*

The story goes that one Sunday morning a maiden from Cromarty was walking along the path next to Loch Slin, when she rounded a corner to see a tall woman in the water cleaning clothes on a rock. Spread across the ground near the woman were more than thirty blood-stained smocks and shirts. The maiden thought it was strange, but carried on her way. It wasn't until later that she realised this sighting occurred shortly before the roof of Fearn Abbey collapsed, killing thirty-six people. This legend is supported by real-life events, as the abbey roof really did collapse in 1742, killing a large number of people.

BLUE MEN OF MINCH

(Also known as: *Storm Kelpies*)

The Blue Men of Minch are mysterious and elusive creatures with blue skin that live in the water between the Isle of Lewis and mainland Scotland. In 1917, the creatures were described in a book called *Wonder Tales from Scottish Myth and Legend* by Donald Alexander Mackenzie, who stated that:

"They are of human size, and they have great strength. By day and by night they swim round and between the Shant Isles, and the sea there is never at rest... The Blue Men wear blue caps and grey faces which appear above the waves that they raise with their long restless arms."

The Blue Men were also known as Storm Kelpies and when not sleeping on top of the waves, they would skim lightly beneath the surface of the water, always on the lookout for unwary sailors so that they may sink their boats and drown their crew. Mackenzie stated that they would splash with mad delight when a storm was brewing, as they knew that they would soon be able to cause mischief.

Some legends say they possessed the power to summon storms on even the calmest of days. They were swift swimmers, moving in a twisting and diving motion similar to a porpoise. They could also speak and were said to compete with boat captains in a battle of poetry, calling out two lines as they approached ships. Should the captain fail to win the poetic sea battle, they would attempt to capsize his boat.

The origins of the Blue Men legends are unknown. Some have suggested they may have been Moorish slaves attempting to escape to freedom, their bodies becoming blue once the cold of the water had taken hold. This would explain the 'splashing around' used to describe their behaviour. Or perhaps the mythical creatures were simply Picts, who would paint their bodies and cross the sea in low-lying boats, which may have looked like blue men rising from beneath the waves.

Or could their riddle have been solved by a modern-day 'blue man'? Paul Karason, an American also known as Papa Smurf, became famous due to his skin turning blue. His condition was the result of a medical condition called argyria, or silver poisoning caused by dietary supplements. Paul drank about 10 ounces of colloidal silver every day, mixed in water. He believed it cured arthritis in his shoulders and his acid reflux issue. Had the people living around the Isle of Lewis at this time took to drinking silver-laced concoctions? Maybe as part of a long-forgotten medicinal or ritual purpose? Or is there yet another explanation offered by modern science?

The Blue Fugates of Kentucky were the result of six generations of a genetic anomaly and inbreeding. The rare blood disorder they carried meant that their skin was blue, due to a lack of oxygenated blood. Both parents need to carry the rare recessive gene responsible, in order to have a blue baby. Could this have been the case then for The Blue Men of Minch? There have certainly been other cases of blue babies being born throughout the world. Until the day the legendary Blue Men of Minch return, this mystery will remain unsolved.

BOOBRIE

The boobrie is a malevolent shapeshifter that lives in the lochs of the west coast of Scotland. The creature normally adopts the form of a huge water bird but is also said to take the shape of other mythical monsters.

Folklorist, Ronald Black, believes the boobrie may have got its name from the word boibhre, which means cow giver (or cow bestowing). However, Scottish lexicographer, Edward Dwelly, states that it may have been derived from the word tarbh-boidhre (commonly tarbh-aoidhre in northern counties) which means a monster, demon or god capable of changing itself into many forms.

It's interesting that Dwelly also defines the singular 'tarbh' as meaning 'bull' because the boobrie has also been known to take the form of the mythical water bull, which we will look at later in this chapter.

The boobrie's favourite food sources are otters, but they have been known to feed on livestock being transported on ships. The boobrie can easily speed across a loch by changing into a water horse which simply gallops across the surface of the water. During the summer months, legend says it will also hunt larger prey, such as horses, by transforming into a giant insect.

In *Popular Tales of the West Highlands*, John Francis Campbell suggests that the legend of the boobrie may actually have been caused by sightings of the great auk, a flightless animal that became extinct in the mid-19th century.

Campbell also suggests that the unique call of the boobrie, which sounds like a bull, may have come from confused witnesses hearing the common bittern, which would visit Scotland on rare occasions.

In *Survivals in Belief Among the Celts*, George Henderson describes the preferred water bird shape normally taken by the boobrie. The creature was said to have a huge, hooked black beak and short, powerful legs that ended in webbed feet with gigantic claws.

Henderson's work also contains a story entitled *boobrie as tarbh uisge*. The legendary tale begins with a man, Eachann, feeding a huge black bull that he had discovered on the brink of death by the edge of Loch nan Dobhran, on the west coast of Argyll.

A few months later, Eachann's girlfriend, Phemie, occassionally senses strange shadows on the loch, which (for some unknown reason) make her think of her former lover, Murdoch.

One evening, Phemie was staying at a sheiling near the loch, daydreaming about her great life with Eachann, when she sensed a foreboding shadow behind her. Turning quickly, she was grabbed by Murdoch, who tied her hands and wrapped her in a blanket.

Just when things were looking bleak for Phemie, she was rescued by a giant water bull, who raced in and knocked Murdoch down. The creature then knelt down and allowed Phemie to ride away on its back until she was safely at her mother's house.

The bull disappeared and was never seen again. But before it left, it called out to Phemie (translated from Gaelic):

'I was assisted by a young man
And I aided a maid in distress;
Then after three hundred years of bondage
Relieve me quickly.'

Another legend, told by John Francis Campbell, describes a hunter who attempted to shoot a boobrie. On a cold day in February, the hunter had spotted the beast on a sea loch. The man waded into the chilly water until it was up to his shoulder. But when he was closing in on the beast, it suddenly dived beneath the water. The brave hunter held his position in the freezing water for forty-five minutes and then waited by the shore for another six hours, but the boobrie never returned.

A third legend, captured by John Gregorson Campbell, tells of a farmer and his son from the Isle of Mull. The two men were ploughing a field near Loch Frisa when one of the horses lost a shoe and the work ground to a halt.

However, the men noticed another horse nearby, which they harnessed as a replacement. All was going well until they came to work the ground nearest the loch. Suddenly the horse became restless and the farmer attempted to encourage the beast to move with the gentle use of his whip. But as the whip landed, the horse let out a mighty bellow and transformed into a gigantic boobrie. The terrified farmer and his son huddled together as the boobrie dived into the loch, pulling the plough and other three horses with it.

CEASG

(Also known as: *maighdean na tuinne* (maid of the wave) or *maighdean mhara* (maid of the sea))

The ceasg is a Scottish mermaid who has the upper body of a beautiful woman and the lower body of a young salmon (grilse). In *Scottish Folk-Lore and Folk Life - Studies in Race, Culture and Tradition,* Donald Mackenzie notes that the ceasg didn't just live in the sea, but also frequented Scotland's rivers and streams. If you were fortunate enough to catch her, the ceasg would grant you three wishes. And if you were extremely lucky, she may even marry you. Mackenzie says that many famous maritime pilots were said to be descended from the union of a ceasg mother and a human father. Eventually, the ceasg would return to the sea, but would always love and watch over their human descendants, protecting them from storms and helping them to fish.

Mackenzie notes that the legends also have a darker side, and the ceasg may be an ancient sea goddess to which humans were sacrificed. In some tales, the ceasg took on a monstrous form and swallowed a brave hero whole, where they remained alive in her stomach. The hero had been promised to the ceasg by his father, but they broke the deal. The hero's wife had to play a harp to soothe the beast so that her husband could escape. Unfortunately, when the wife stops playing the ceasg wakes up and swallows her. This means the hero must seek the help of a wizard, who tells him to obtain an egg that contains the mermaid's life force. The hero finds the egg, rescues his wife and kills the ceasg by crushing the egg.

CIREIN-CRÒIN

(Also known as: *ceirean* or *cionarain-crò*)

The cirein-cròin is a gigantic sea monster who was capable of eating seven whales at a time, but could also disguise itself as a small, silver fish.

In *Gaelic names of beasts (mammalia), birds, fishes, insects, reptiles, etc.*, Alexander Forbes states that the mythical monster took on the disguise of a smaller fish to tempt fishermen to catch it. But once on board the fisherman's boat, the creature would revert to its true form, destroying the boat and eating the fisherman.

An old Gaelic saying goes:

Seven herrings, a salmon's fill,
Seven salmon, a seal's fill,
Seven seals, a large whale's fill,
Seven whales, a cirein-cròin's fill.

Forbes theorises that the creature may have been a large sea serpent or even a dinosaur. He concludes:

'It is not known what this monster animal was, though it may well have been one of these "Giant fish-destroyers," so ably, inter alia, described by Dr Carmichael McIntosh, which waged war in sea and on land against all and sundry as well as against each other, viz., the gigantic Deinosaurs, some of which, notably the Atlantosaurus, reached to one hundred feet in length with a height of thirty feet, and proportionately awful of aspect.'

EACH-UISGE

(Also known as: *each-uisce* or *cabyll-ushtey*)

The each-uisge is a Scottish water horse which resembled a kelpie but was a much more malevolent creature. Katharine Briggs describes the each-uisge as one of the most dangerous of all the water horses. The each-uisge lived in the sea, sea lochs, and fresh water lochs, but would shapeshift and come onto land in the form of a huge bird, a horse or even a handsome man.

Briggs states that, while in horse form, the each-uisge could be safely mounted and ridden. But should the beast get even a momentary glimpse (or sniff) of water, then its skin would become a powerful adhesive, trapping the rider in place and drowning them in the deepest part of the loch. The each-uisge would then tear the poor rider to shreds and devour every part, except the liver, which it allowed to float to the surface.

When the each-uisge walked the land as a handsome man, the only way you could tell it was a legendary creature was by spotting the unusual amount of sand, mud and weeds in its hair. These beliefs led to Highland communities being wary of animals and strangers lingering alone near lochs.

The legendary Irish water horse (aughisky) bears a strong resemblance to the Scottish myths, as it would also come onto land in the form of a horse. William Butler Yeats noted that if you could harness the beast and keep it away from water, it would make the finest of all steeds.

The book *More West Highland Tales*, by John Francis Campbell, says that one way to lure the Scottish each-uisge out of the water was with the smell of roasting meat and contains a legend that makes use of this knowledge:

One day the daughter of a blacksmith from Raasay was eaten by the creature. Mad with grief, the blacksmith and his son sought vengeance, so they forged a set of great hooks. By the loch, they roasted a sheep and heated the hooks until they glowed red hot.

Suddenly a mist appeared over the loch, and the mythical monster burst from the water and devoured the sheep. But as it did so, the blacksmith and his son pierced its flesh with their hooks, trapping the creature in place until they killed it. The following morning, the beast's body had dissolved into a jelly-like substance.

John Gregorson Campbell also recounted many legends about the each-uisge. In one tale, a young boy had touched the water horse and was being dragged into the water but was able to save himself by chopping off his own finger. In another, a man was also able to save himself from a watery fate by placing his feet on either side of a narrow gate as the beast ran towards the loch, thus ripping himself free of the creature's sticky hide.

A Highland freebooter (pirate-like adventurer) once met the each-uisge in its human form and had recognised the mythical creature for what it was. The freebooter found that his normal bullets weren't able to damage the beast, but when he loaded his gun with a silver coin, he was able to drive the each-uisge back into the water.

Campbell states that the each-uisge would appear as a handsome male because it was particularly fond of both mating with and eating human women.

In one legend, a young woman is herding cattle when she meets a handsome young man. Quickly becoming friendly, the woman rests a while and allows the man to lay his head on her lap and fall asleep.

It was only when the man stretched himself out that she noticed he had hooves instead of feet and sand in his hair, so she gently laid him on the ground and ran away.

There are many other tales of the creature's amorous advances towards fair maidens, including the time the beast (in human form) knocked on a woman's door and tried to seduce her, but instead received a pan of boiling water thrown between his legs, causing him to flee in pain.

That each-uisge was still luckier than his unfortunate counterpart who was ambushed by a father and three sons as he attempted to charm the daughter. The poor creature reverted to its horse form and tried to escape to the loch and drown its attackers, but was killed by the daggers of the girl's protective family before it could reach the water's edge.

In Folklore from the Hebrides, Malcolm MacPhail describes a knoll on the Isle of Lewis that lies near the freshwater Loch a' Mhuileinn (Loch of the Mill). The mound is known as Cnoc-na-Bèist (Hillock of the Monster) and it was named after an each-uisge who was slain there by the brother of a woman it tried to seduce.

FINFOLK

(Also known as: *Finnfolk, Finman* and *Finwife*)

The Finfolk is a race of mysterious shapeshifters who terrorise the shores of the Orkney Islands. Practitioners of dark magic, the Finfolk would regularly swim from their underwater haven of Finfolkaheem (Finfolk's Home) to the waters around Orkney, in search of human captives.

The Finfolk would spend the cold winters at their ancestral home of Finfolkaheem and on the mythical island of Hildaland (Hidden Land), waiting for the warmer spring and summer months to stalk the Orcadian beaches. Both the Finman (male) and Finwife (female) would be on the hunt for careless fishermen or distracted youths near the shore. Once captured, their victims would be forced to serve the Finfolk as their spouses.

In order to abduct their life partner, the Finwife would often appear as a beautiful mermaid with long, golden hair and sing with a voice said to be as wonderful as that of the Greek Sirens. The Finmen had to work a little harder to capture their brides, often disguising themselves as harmless sea animals, plants or even discarded clothing as they floated closer to their prey. Sometimes a Finman would even pose as a human fisherman, with their bottom half hidden inside a row boat.

The Finfolk were known to be particularly greedy and it was said that if you were captured by one, you should throw some silver coins or jewellery into the water and make your escape while the creatures were distracted.

The *Orkneyjar* website, which captures some of the folklore and heritage of the Orkney Islands, has a number of tales about the legend of the Finfolk.

The reason for the Finfolk choosing human life partners is that, if a Finwife marries a Finman, she is cursed to lose all her beauty and mystical charm. As long as she remains unmarried to a human, every seven years the Finwife grows uglier until she eventually becomes the creature known as the Finwife Hag.

Therefore, it's desirable for a Finwife to find a human husband as quickly as possible, while she still has her youth and beauty. This practice by the females of the species in turn forces the Finman to find a human wife to share his life with.

The Finwives who fail to capture a human husband, and marry a Finman instead, are forced to go onto land and use their powers and skills to find work as healers or spinners. All the silver the Finwife earns from these chores must be sent home to her husband, or she will be severely beaten. Her one solace from this life is the company of a black cat, who has the power to shape-shift into a fish so that she can deliver messages to her family back home.

When a Finwife successfully finds a human male she usually drags her new man to live with her in Finfolkaheem. It's said that this underwater home is a huge city, with gigantic crystal halls and ornate water gardens decorated with seaweed of every colour. Nights in Finfolkaheem are lit by the phosphorescent glow of tiny sea creatures.

While the legends describe Finfolkaheem in vivid detail, much less is known about Hildaland, the secret island retreat of the Finfolk.

Hildaland was said to be a paradise for the mythical creatures, where even the stern, gloomy-faced Finmen allowed their tall and thin bodies to relax, once they had abducted a human wife, of course.

The strong Finmen were said to be powerful sorcerers who could row between Orkney and Norway in only seven oar-strokes, as well as making their boats invisible, or even create an armada of phantom boats to confuse their enemies.

The Finmen were very territorial and would use their powers to destroy any human fishing boats that strayed into their waters. Local fishermen were said to draw a Christian cross on the bottom of their boats with chalk or tar to ward off Finfolk attacks.

Once the Finman had caught his soon-to-be-wife, she had no chance to escape. It's said that no human man or woman ever returned from Hildaland. This was partly due to the island being either invisible, hidden below the surface, or surrounded by a magical fog that would turn sailors around.

The real-life island of Eynhallow (Holy Isle) is said to be the fabled Hildaland, once the island had been cleansed by the Goodman of Thorodale and his sons with salt and crosses carved into the land, thus losing its magical powers and causing the Finfolk to abandon it forever.

FUATH

(Also known as: *arrachd, fuath-arrachd, vough* or *vaugh*. Plural: *fuathan*)

The fuathan is a category of (mainly) water spirits who haunt the Scottish Highlands. Folklorist Donald Mackenzie classifies the Fuath as malevolent creatures who chiefly inhabit Scotland's seas, rivers and lochs.

John Gregorson Campbell recognises the fuathan are mainly water spirits, but also contain a few creatures of the land, particularly dark-inclined spectres and goblins.

In *The Folklore Journal*, Charlotte H. Dempster agrees that the fuathan represent a broad category of evil and dangerous mythical beasts.

In their respective works, Campbell and Dempster both gathered a number of folklore tales about the fuath. In some stories, a fuath marries a human and their children are born with a mane and tail, like that of a lion.

This led to a third folklorist, John Francis Campbell, broadly ascribing these traits to the fuathan, particularly because there was evidence that these traits (in some form) had indeed occurred in some members of the Munroe family. The locals whispered that an ancestor of the Munroe family had mated with a fuath many generations before. This sweeping generalisation of the fuathan having manes and tails was later disproved by the folklore tales of John Gregorson Campbell and Charlotte H. Dempster.

In one of those tales, there was a mill in Sutherland that belonged to the Dempster family estate (known as Skibo). This mill sat alongside a stream that ran from Loch Migdale and was known as Moulin na Vaugha/Fouadh (Mill of the Fuath) because it was haunted by a fuath and her son, the brollachan. The fuath was said to be a noseless banshee with long yellow hair who wore a green silk dress, a traditional colour for fuath in that area. However, a gamekeeper from the family estate also claimed to have seen a spectral woman in a golden silk dress leaping into the River Shin.

The story goes that the fuath would transform into an amorphous jellyfish-like mass when a light was shone on it and was eventually captured through the use of steel objects, in particular an awl and sewing needles. Some accounts also tell of a fuath who lived on the Dempster estate who had webbed feet, but it's unknown if this was the same creature. The fuath's son has his own mythical tale, known as *The Brollachan*. The legend goes that the brollachan was a shapeless blob that still possessed eyes and a mouth, but was only capable of saying two phrases, *mi-phrein* and *tu-phrein* (*myself* and *yourself*). Folklorists believe that the creature's larval form is due to him being young and having not yet learned to maintain a fixed form, like his mother.

One day a crippled alms-receiving man ('Allay na Moulin' Murray) came across the brollachan laying at the mill. The man was said to have stoked the fire with peat until it burned the brollachan. However, the creature's lack of vocabulary meant it wasn't able to tell its mother who had caused its burns.

The brollachan was attacked because, if given the chance, it would possess the body of any creature large enough to hold its form, including humans. In folklore wisdom, you could tell when a brollachan had possessed an animal or human because their skin colour would become darker, their eyes glowed red and they flung themselves around in a wild manner. Humans could only survive for a few days before the brollachan used up all their life force.

A second legend exists that involves another (possibly the same) brollachan at the same mill on the Dempster family estate. Once again, a steel awl and sewing needle are the weapons of choice for a man from Inveran who made a bet with a friend that he could go and capture the 'kelpie' of the mill. The man is successful, thanks in part to the black-muzzled dog that accompanied him. He tied the kelpie to his horse and made his way home. However, while crossing the burn at the south of Loch Migdale, the creature begins to grow agitated. The man pokes it with both the awl and the needle and the monster cries out that the needle is worse. When he returned home, his friends shone a light on the horse and the kelpie dropped to the ground, a shapeless lump, winning the man his wager.

Legends of the fuath, and the brollachan in particular, served a greater purpose in our cultural history. The scary tales of these creatures taught children not to wander too far from home, or play in dark or watery places. They were also a warning against trusting strangers or approaching animals that were acting strangely (and which may have had a disease, such as rabies). My favourite brollachan was the digital beast with a thirst for knowledge who would emerge from walls in the television show *Knightmare*.

KELPIE

The kelpie is arguably the second most widely-known mythical monster in Scotland, just behind the Loch Ness Monster (who we will meet in a moment). So revered are these mythical water horses that located between Falkirk and Grangemouth you will find gigantic 30-metre (100ft) tall horse-head sculptures dedicated to *The Kelpies.*

The kelpie is a shape-shifting water spirit that, given the sheer number of legends, appears to live in just about every body of water in the whole of Scotland (and beyond). It's theorised that the word kelpie may have originated from the Gaelic *calpa* or *cailpeach*, meaning *heifer* or *colt.*

The word is hundreds of years old and an ode by William Collins dating from before 1759 is the first known use of the term kelpie (spelt kaelpie) to describe a mythical creature. However, *A Dictionary of the Older Scottish Tongue* lists Kelpie hoall and Kelpie hooll as place names from the 1674 burgh records for Kirkcudbright.

Kelpies are often described as being powerful black horse-like creatures that prefer to live in the deep pools of rivers and streams. It's said that the kelpie's hooves are reversed and it retains these hooves when transforming into human form, usually that of a handsome man. Some folklorists and Christian writers believe it has these traits due to its association as a servant of Satan.

The evidence of this, they say, can be found in the 1786 poem *Address to the Deil* (*Devil*) by Robert Burns, which contains the lines:

'When thowes dissolve the snawy hoord
An' float the jinglin icy boord
Then, Water-kelpies haunt the foord,
By your direction,
An' nighted Trav'llers are allur'd
To their destruction.'

The legends of the kelpies is one of the most debated topics within Scottish folklore as many researchers believe that the term kelpie (and its various anglicised spellings) were used broadly to describe a wide range of creatures with similar traits.

In *The Lore of Scotland: A Guide to Scottish Legends*, Jennifer Westwood and Sophia Kingshill suggest that early transcribers of folklore tales also caused the inverse to occur, as they used a wide range of names to describe the same creature.

This can be seen in the similarities between the kelpie and other legendary creatures, such the Welsh *ceffyl dŵr*, the Manx *cabbyl-ushtey*, the American *wihwin*, the Australian *bunyip*, the Germanic *nixe* and the Scandinavian *bäckahäst*. Even within Scotland itself, the kelpie bears a strong resemblance to the *nuggles* and *shoopiltees* of Shetland and the *tangies* of Orkney.

In 1929, folklorist Joseph McKenzie McPherson noted that kelpies from Aberdeenshire appeared as horses with a unique mane of serpents and that the kelpie in the River Spey was actually white, not black, and would sing to entice people onto its back.

These disparities may also explain why folklorists have sometimes disagreed over the kelpie's habitat and behaviours. One distinction suggested between kelpies and the similar each-uisge discussed earlier is that the kelpie haunts streams and rivers, but the each-uisge haunts lochs. However, Sir Walter Scott has suggested that kelpies may also reside in some lochs. Perhaps we may never fully unravel all the historical distinctions and translations, but instead can be entertained by the legendary stories of the creature that play such a large part in Scottish heritage.

Similar to the each-uisge, kelpie myths usually involve the creature attempting to mate with or devour humans. It also employs similar methods as the each-uisge, by tempting people to ride on its back, or transforming into an attractive male. One such tale, told by Heather McNeil, takes place on the island of Barra, in the Outer Hebrides, where a kelpie attempts to seduce a beautiful girl and make her his wife. However, the girl recognises the signs that this strange man is really a kelpie and removes his silver necklace while he sleeps. This causes the kelpie to transform back into its horse-like form and the girl leads the creature to her father's farm, where the kelpie is forced to toil in the fields for a year.

One day, the girl is advised by a wise man to return the silver necklace (now in bridle form) to the kelpie. When she does so, the kelpie changes back into the handsome man she had first met. The wise man asked the kelpie if he would rather be a kelpie or a mortal. The kelpie turns to the girl and asks her if she would marry him in his human form. The girl says yes, the kelpie becomes a mortal human and they soon become husband and wife.

Sometimes, the kelpie (in its equine form, a very important distinction here) would mate with a normal horse. It's said that the offspring of this mating are short and sturdy horses who cannot drown.

On the border between Kincardineshire and Forfarshire, near St Cyrus, there used to be a village called Morphie. One day the Laird of Morphie captured a kelpie and forced the creature to carry huge stones so that the laird could build a large home. Although the laird released the kelpie once the work was complete, the mythical monster sought revenge for its forced labour and cursed the laird with:

'Sair back and sair banes,
Drivin' the Laird o' Morphies's stanes,
The Laird o' Morphie'll never thrive,
As lang's the kelpy is alive.'

All that remains of this fabled village and large home today is a farmhouse called Morphie.

Many legends tell of a group of boys who would climb onto a kelpie's back, while their friend watched from the shore. The child riding at the front of the water horse reaches down to stroke its neck, but suddenly its skin becomes adhesive and sticks the boys to its back. In the tales, the boy cuts off either his finger or his hand to escape, but his friends are dragged beneath the water, their entrails later found floating on the surface. *Tales of the Water-Kelpie*, published in *Celtic Magazine*, suggests that it was a Highland lad from Thurso whose antics first spawned this legend.

Folklorist, Derek Gath Whitley, suggested that kelpie legends may have originated from horse sacrifices in ancient Scandinavia. Alternatively, similar to the fuath, the tales may have acted as a warning for children against the dangers of water, and for women against the perils of strange men.

A further suggestion, proposed by Charles Milton Smith, is that waterspouts would form on Scottish lochs and give the impression of movement as they glided across its surface. This idea is supported by Sir Walter Scott, who suggests that *The Lady of the Lake* myth may also have similar origins, in his poem of the same name:

'The desert gave him visions wild,
Such as might suit the spectre's child.
Where with black cliffs the torrents toil,
He watched the wheeling eddies boil,
Jill from their foam his dazzled eyes
Beheld the River Demon rise:
The mountain mist took form and limb
Of noontide hag or goblin grim;'

In another legend, told in an 1889 issue of *The Folk-Lore Journal*, a man is attempting to cross a deep river to reach his dying wife but is dismayed to discover a rainstorm has washed away the bridge. A stranger approaches him and offers to carry him across the river. The man sees that this stranger is wearing clothes that are wet up to the armpits, so assumes he must know a path across and agrees to his offer of help. However, halfway across, the stranger attempts to throw the man from his shoulders into the raging river.

The man clings on and the pair struggle in the water until they are swept downstream to a shallow shore. Back on solid ground, the man escapes with his life. The enraged kelpie launches a giant rock after the man, which later becomes known as the 'kelpie stone' and locals would add more rocks beside it until it formed a cairn.

As well as its more famous cousin, Loch Ness also has a number of kelpie legends attached to it. In *Folklore of Scottish Lochs and Springs*, James M. Mackinlay recounts the tale of a brave Highlander, MacGrigor, who once cornered a kelpie that had been terrorising the woods and shores of the loch in the early 19th century. MacGrigor took the beast by surprise and cut off its bridle, without which the kelpie would die within twenty-four hours. The creature, who was able to speak, attempted to bargain with the Highlander, following him back to his home. Once there, the kelpie told MacGrigor that he wouldn't be able to enter his house while holding the bridle, as there was a large cross above the door. MacGrigor simply laughed and tossed the bridle through an open window, sealing the kelpie's fate.

MacGrigor's legend doesn't end there though, as it's said that the magical bridle was then passed down through his family. In *Scottish Charms and Amulets*, George F. Black says that the Willox's Ball and Bridle, as it came to be known, was believed to have healing powers. All one had to do was place the bridle in water and chant the spell (or prayer) 'In the name of the Father, the Son and of the Holy Ghost' and the water would then take on magical healing properties, similar to holy water.

While removing its magical bridle may cause a kelpie to die within a day, one of the suggested ways to instantly kill a kelpie is with a silver bullet. In *The Magic Arts in Celtic Britain*, Lewis Spence includes an account of a kelpie being shot with a silver bullet which reduced the mythical creature to a jellyfish-like blob.

Iron weapons, a common anti-evil weapon in folktales, may also be effective against the beast. Folklorist, Gary R. Varner, states that frequent appearances by a kelpie were scaring a blacksmith's family at their summer cottage. To protect his family, the blacksmith forged a pair of sharp iron spears, which he heated in a fire and used to attack the creature's body. The blacksmith succeeded in piercing the kelpie's hide, reducing it to a 'heap of starch'.

Given that the majority of human settlements were first formed near a water source, it would appear that kelpie legends come from a time when warnings and lessons in story form were necessary, as the majority of the population was unlikely to be able to swim. It was easy to keep children away from the water while parents were in church on Sundays, with a simple tale about the dangerous creature that lived there. The howling or wailing of a kelpie may have been a real-life warning that the wind had whipped up and a storm was approaching. Stories of a kelpie's tail sounding like thunder when it hit the water, so you should never go there, kept many people safe from being out in the open (or standing under trees near the loch) during storms, where they may be struck by lightning. Despite their deadly reputation, kelpie legends may actually have saved many lives over the years.

LAVELLAN

(Also known as: *làbh-allan*, *la-mhalan* or *la-bhallan*)

The lavellan is a type of water rodent that lives in deep pools and rivers. The Scottish Gaelic name làbh-allan is used for water shrew and water vole, as well as being applied to the mythical creature.

In Edward Dwelly's Scottish Gaelic dictionary, the highly toxic lavellan is described as being much larger than the common rat. Legends say that the creature was able to spread its poison in such a manner that it could injure cattle that were over one hundred feet away.

In 1828, Scottish minister and naturalist, John Fleming, suggested that the general dislike that people felt towards the common ermine, a type of weasel, was caused by the disdain they held for the mythical lavellan, which was a widely held belief in Caithness at that time.

Rob Donn, the Scottish Gaelic poet from Sutherland, mentions the mythical monster in his work. The Welsh naturalist, Thomas Pennant, enquired about the lavellan while conducting his research. Pennant discovered that locals would hunt and capture the water rodent in order to preserve its skin.

When any of their working animals became sick, they would dip the lavellan's skin in water, which gave the liquid healing qualities. They would then have their sick animals drink the water, after which they would become fully healed.

LOCH NESS MONSTER

(Affectionately known as: *Nessie.* Scottish Gaelic: *Uilebheist Loch Nis*)

The Loch Ness Monster is one of the most famous mythical monsters in the world and, even to this day, remains one of Scotland's most enduring mysteries.

Nessie, as the legendary creature is commonly known, is reported to reside in Loch Ness, which is 23 miles (37 kilometres) southwest of Inverness, in the Scottish Highlands. The deep, freshwater loch has a surface area of 22 square miles (56 square kilometres), and is 755 feet (230 metres) deep.

This makes Loch Ness the second-largest loch by surface area, after Loch Lomond; the second deepest in Scotland, after Loch Morar; and the largest by volume in the whole of Great Britain. Plenty of room then, to hide a mythical monster.

Sightings of the creature have reported a large, dinosaur-like monster with a long neck and one or more humps protruding from the water. The first recorded sighting of Nessie was nearly 1,500 years ago when an unfortunate farmer was apparently eaten by a large beast erupting from Loch Ness.

In 1934, the legend gained momentum when a London doctor produced a photograph that appeared to show Nessie protruding from the water.

There have been many more sightings over the years, despite the British Broadcasting Corporation (BBC) completing an extensive search of the loch in 2003. Using 600 sonar beams and satellite tracking, the BBC appeared to have concluded that Nessie was a myth. Yet in summer 2021 a number of newspapers reported that official Nessie sightings were on the rise.

Lots of previous sightings have been shown to be hoaxes and Robert Todd Carroll, author of *The Skeptic's Dictionary: A Collection of Strange Beliefs, Amusing Deceptions and Dangerous Delusions*, states that all reports of the creature are based on hoaxes and the misidentification of mundane objects, particularly from poor quality photographs. Regardless, the sheer number of sightings makes an intriguing story.

The very first reported sighting from 1,500 years ago appears in *Life of St Columba*, by Adomnán, who wrote that the Irish Monk, Saint Columba, was travelling with his companions through the lands of the Picts when they met some locals burying a man near to the River Ness. The group explained that the man had been a victim of the great water beast that lived in the loch.

On hearing their tale, Saint Columba sent one of his followers, Luigne moccu Min, to swim across the river. Suddenly the beast rose from the water and went to attack his follower. However, Saint Columba made the sign of the cross and said to the creature 'Go no further. Do not touch the man. Go back at once.' The beast fled and Saint Columba was credited with performing a miracle.

In 1934, the *Inverness Courier* reported that D. Mackenzie of Balnain sent a letter to Rupert Gould, one of the early investigators into the Loch Ness Monster, stating that many years earlier (circa 1871/72) they had spotted an object similar to a log, or an upturned boat, moving and churning up the water.

In his book *Loch Ness Monster*, Tim Dinsdale tells of another sighting, this time in 1888, by a mason called Alexander Macdonald of Abriachan who had witnessed a large, stubby-legged animal swimming in the loch that resembled a huge salamander. Concerned for the safety of local residents, Macdonald reported the incident to the Loch Ness water bailiff at that time, Alex Campbell.

Descriptions of Nessie in its popular modern form began on 22nd July 1933, when George Spicer and his wife saw a huge animal slide across the road in front of their car and enter the loch. The couple reported the creature as being about 4 feet (1.2 m) high and 25 feet (8 m) long, with a long, narrow neck that resembled an elephant's trunk.

In the same year, a photograph was taken by Hugh Gray, who was walking his dog near Foyers and happened to capture a blurred image of the creature. However, upon the 1963 discovery of two lantern slides by Dr Maurice Burton, which were contact positives from the original negative, it was thought to simply be an otter splashing about in the water.

In 1934, a motorcyclist and veterinary student, Arthur Grant, was cruising around the north-eastern end of the loch, near Abriachan, when he nearly drove straight into the mythical monster. He described his sudden encounter as a near-collision with a huge creature with a long neck and a small head, which looked like a cross between a plesiosaur and a seal. Grant watched in wonder as the beast slid across the road and entered the loch. Upon following, all that remained were ripples. Upon seeing a sketch of the creature created by Grant, Dr Maurice Burton once again disproved this sighting as merely being the resemblance and behaviour of an otter.

1934 was a big turning point in the Nessie legend, as one of the most famous photographs of the creature emerged. The 'surgeon's photograph' was reportedly taken by Robert Kenneth Wilson, a London general surgeon and gynaecologist. The photograph achieved widespread interest when it was published in the *Daily Mail*. The image shows the small head and back of a dinosaur-like creature.

The photograph attracted much interest and debate until it was largely disproved as a hoax in 1993 when newer technology allowed a more in-depth analysis. It is now considered to have been created with a toy submarine built by Christian Spurling, the son-in-law of Marmaduke Wetherell who confessed to the hoax before he died, and proved by a small white dot that appears to be towing the submarine in every photo. Wetherell had been ridiculed by his employer, the *Daily Mail*, for reporting Nessie footprints that were later proved to be a hoax. Fortunately for Wetherell, his son-in-law, Spurling, just happened to be a talented sculpture specialist. Their friend Maurice Chambers passed the photographic plates on to Wilson, who then claimed the photographs as his own and sold them to the *Daily Mail*. The newspaper then announced the 'evidence' of the monster that they had ridiculed Wetherell for previously.

In 1938, a South African tourist, G. E. Taylor, filmed something moving within the loch. Dr Maurice Burton was once again on hand to dismiss the evidence as being an object, rather than an animal. That same year, growing interest in Nessie led to the chief constable of Inverness-shire writing a letter in which he said he might not be able to protect the creature (which he stated definitely existed) after discovering a group of hunters armed with a harpoon gun.

In 1954, the crew of a fishing boat took sonar readings of the loch and noticed a large object 479 feet (146 metres) below them that was keeping pace with their boat for around 2,600 feet (800 metres), before disappearing. In 1958, the *Weekly Scotsman* published a photograph that had been taken three years earlier by Peter MacNab. The image showed two distinct black humps on the loch, but the original negative was later found by the author, Roy Mackal, to differ from the published image and likely a hoax.

In 1960, aeronautical engineer (and later the *Loch Ness Monster* author), Tim Dinsdale, appeared to have filmed the creature, but when the contrast was increased it was revealed to look a lot like a man in a boat. However, in 1993 a documentary called *Loch Ness Discovered* digitally enhanced Dinsdale's film footage. In doing so, they actually discovered a previously unnoticed body of a large creature, hidden beneath the surface.

In 1977, Anthony 'Doc' Shiels (a psychic and magician) released a photograph that became known as the Loch Ness Muppet, due to its obviously staged nature. In 2007, a video was taken by Gordon Holmes which showed a long, black creature moving quickly through the water. It attracted lots of attention from Scottish news outlets, but a marine biologist at the Loch Ness 2000 Centre, Adrian Shine, said that, while he recognised it was some of the best footage ever captured of the Loch Ness Monster, it was more likely to be an otter, seal or water bird.

In 2011, a Loch Ness boat captain, Marcus Atkinson, captured a sonar image of a 4.9 feet (1.5 metres) wide underwater object that appeared to follow his boat for two minutes. However, scientists from the National Oceanography Centre believed this to simply be a bloom of zooplankton or algae. In 2012, another boat captain and veteran Nessie hunter, George Edwards, released a photograph he had taken the previous year. It appeared to show Nessie's three humps but suggested in news interviews that it was possibly three separate monsters. Steve Feltham, a Loch Ness researcher, pointed out that it looked a lot like a fibreglass hump used in a documentary in which Edwards had featured. In 2013, Edwards admitted it was all a hoax.

In 2013, a man from East Kilbride took a five-minute video of strange waves emanating from a mysterious black object just below the surface of the loch. David Elder had been taking a picture of a swan when he noticed the strange phenomenon. In 2014, Apple Maps appeared to show a satellite image of a 98 feet (30 metres) shape in Loch Ness.

Numerous searches of the loch have taken place over the years, using all manner of technology. Many consider the 2003 hunt by the BBC to have been the death of the Nessie myth, as the 600 sonar beams and powerful satellite tracking used in the search found zero evidence of any monster. However, one of the most interesting results comes from a 2018 DNA survey conducted by researchers from universities around the world. The researchers discovered that there was no otter or seal DNA in the loch, which goes against previous explanations of Nessie photographs, including those provided by Dr Maurice Burton. A lot of eel DNA was found, but no reptilian DNA. Everyone can make their own mind up about what these results may mean for the existence of and explanations for the Loch Ness Monster.

There have been many varied explanations for Nessie sightings, including it simply being an optical illusion caused by human psychology. This was proposed by Ronald Binns, who says humans simply see what they expect to see, creating a sociological phenomenon. Other explanations have been attributed to a vast menagerie of animals and the ripples they cause on the loch, including birds, eels, sharks, elephants and catfish. Even a number of inanimate objects have been blamed for the Nessie legend, such as trees, branches, logs, wave and water effects, and even seismic gas caused by earthquakes.

Whether you believe in the existence of the legendary creature or not, Nessie remains a significant part of Scottish culture that continues to draw the intrigue of researchers, the ire of sceptics and the love of tourists from around the world, to a beautiful Scottish loch.

MORAG

(Scottish Gaelic: *Mòrag*)

Morag is a terrifying monster that reportedly haunts Loch Morar, in Lochaber. In *Alien Animals*, Janet and Colin Bord describe accounts of the creature, which is said to closely resemble the Loch Ness Monster.

It's said that Morag was named after the loch it frequents and the earliest sighting of the creature date back to 1887. In 1981 there were thirty-four recorded sightings of Morag, with sixteen of those incidents being witnessed by multiple people at the same time.

One of the most widely reported sightings was by two local men, Duncan McDonell and William Simpson, who had been enjoying a day out on the loch in their boat.

As they were manoeuvring around the water, one of the men accidentally struck a large creature with his oar. Finding themselves suddenly under attack by the enraged beast, McDonell fought with his oar, while Simpson fired at the creature with his rifle.

The two men described Morag as roughly 25 to 30 feet long (7.6 to 9.1 metres), with rough, brown skin. They claimed they saw three dorsal humps rise out of the water and the head of the beast was around a foot (30 centimetres) wide.

After Simpson fired his weapon, the creature sank below the surface and the men escaped from the loch.

MUC-SHEILCH

(Also known as: *Muc-sheilche*)

The Muc-sheilch is another loch monster that is thought to be a distant cousin of the Loch Ness Monster, but with its own distinctive look. The Muc-sheilch lived in Loch Maree, in Wester Ross, but was said to travel to other nearby lochs. This reputation of the wandering creature led to Mr Banks from Letterewe attempting to drain Loch-na-Bèiste, near Aultbea, in the 1850s in search of the mythical monster. Despite the great personal expense invested by Mr Banks, he was unable to fully drain the loch. Interestingly, this attempt was also the basis of the creature being seen as unique from other loch monsters.

Loch-na-Bèiste is Scottish Gaelic for 'loch of the beast'. The word 'beast' was often used in Ireland to describe loch monsters and 'bèiste' is sometimes translated as 'turtle-pig'. This suggests that the creature was a stranger-looking animal than the sleek, eel-like loch monsters from similar legends. For some reason, Mr Banks not only believed in the existence of the Muc-sheilch, but was seemingly offended by it inhabiting the loch. He attempted to poison the beast by filling the loch with quicklime (a substance also known as burnt lime or calcium oxide). This substance reaches temperatures of up to 150 degrees Celsius when placed in water, with many people believing it was the main ingredient in Greek fire, an incendiary weapon used by the Byzantine Empire to set fire to enemy ships. Unfortunately, even armed with this ancient flamethrower fuel, Mr Banks was still unable to reveal the mythical monster within the loch.

NUCKELAVEE

(Alternative spelling: *Nuckalavee*)

The nuckelavee is a grotesque half-horse demon that inhabits the water around the Orkney Islands. It's known to be one of the most evil of all the water-dwelling creatures, with folklorist Katharine Briggs calling it 'the nastiest' demon in the north of Scotland.

In my collection of Scottish short stories, *Mysteries and Misadventures: Tales from the Highlands*, I wrote a story containing a nuckelavee.

In the tale, entitled *Call of the Nuckelavee*, a lone woman walks the sandy dunes of an Orkney beach, following the voice of her drowned father. With her mind full of questions, she spies a dog ahead that appears to be beckoning her to follow. She realises it's her father's dog, missing since the day of his death. Launching herself into the sea after the dog, she comes face to face with the legendary creature that has haunted her nightmares. And she must decide quickly how far she is willing to go to get answers...

Descriptions of the nuckelavee are rare and vary in detail, from early Latin descriptions of Orcadian sea demons to the horse-like monster seen in the modern fantasy genre. When writing about *Orkney Folklore and Sea Legends*, Walter Traill Dennison collated a number of descriptions, including calling the nuckelavee a solitary creature with extremely evil powers, intent on spreading its malevolent influence throughout the islands.

Nobody knows what form the creature takes while it is in the sea, but as soon as it decides to come onto land, it becomes a disgusting centaur-like demon. Dennison tells of the only eye-witness account from a survivor of the beast, Tammas, who said it has a human male torso attached to the body of a horse. However, the rider has no legs, creating a single creature seamlessly stitched together, with giant arms that dragged along the ground. The demon's huge head contained an enormous mouth that released toxic vapour. A single eye glowed red in the centre of its forehead. The most gruesome aspect of the nuckelavee is that it has no skin. Its entire body is a mass of muscle, sinew and bone, exposed to the salty water. The creature faced by the lone woman in my *Call of the Nuckelavee* story was described in line with this traditional narrative:

'It stood three times the height of a man. A colossal horse's head with a single glaring red eye that pierced through the darkness. Upon its back was a man-shaped creature, though where horse ended and rider began she couldn't tell, their bodies fused in a sickening twist of melded sinew. Great clawed hands hung at the end of long arms that skimmed the surface of the water. One claw gripped the remains of what once had been a dog, now decaying and bloated by the sea.

She staggered back, her scream lost in the howl of the wind. She had seen this creature in the books of myths and legends. She recognised its face from half-recalled nightmares.

The nuckelavee.

The skinless creature paced towards her, moonlight reflecting off bare muscle and bleached bone. The pungent smell of sulphur and decay emanated from the beast. With every step, its body pulsed in a disgusting mimicry of a foul tide.

She took another step back, the water now lapping at her waist.

The rider's face split open to reveal two rows of long sharp teeth. A voice called to her. No longer her father's, but the sound of a thousand tortured souls crying out as one.

Come to me.

She dared another step back.

A deafening howl rang out as the creature reared up onto its hind legs, then slammed its hooves back down into the water. It moved towards her, faster now.

She stumbled as her foot caught on a rock.'

The name nuckelavee is thought to have originated from the Orcadian knoggelvi, which Dennison believes means 'Devil of the Sea'. It's considered to be similar to the mukkelevi sea devil that haunts the shores of Shetland and antiquarian, Samuel Hibbert, suggested that the 'nuck' aspect of the name is derived from Old Nick, which is a name attributed to the Devil in Christianity.

Orcadian residents were terrified of the nuckelavee, who was kept in confinement during the summer months by the Mither o' the Sea but was unleashed the rest of the year. It was widely known that if you spoke the creature's name, you must quickly follow it with a prayer of protection. If you came face-to-face with the dreaded demon, you could escape by finding a freshwater river or stream, which the creature would not cross. The demon would also not emerge from the sea if it was raining.

Dennison states that the smoke from burning seaweed would enrage the nuckelavee, which would attack the island residents by emitting toxic vapours that wilted their crops and sickened their animals. The demon would be blamed for everything, from diseased horses to poor harvest and drought. The mythology of the Orkney Islands contains a number of Scandinavian elements and the creature's behaviour was often used to explain natural phenomena that were not yet understood, as well as a warning about the dangers of the sea.

In my book *Mysteries and Misadventures: Tales from the Highlands*, the fearsome nuckelavee is closing in on its prey, when another legendary creature intervenes:

'The horse head snorted as the creature stalked a few steps closer. Its single red eye fixed on its prey.

"Why," she screamed, regaining her footing. "Why us?"

A familiar laugh cut across the gap between them.

With a gentle splash, the surface of the water broke to the left of the creature.

The rider turned its head, its mouth gaping with a threatening roar.

A small black head with large round eyes watched her as it bobbed on the water. With a low growl, it dived beneath the surface again, the moonlight dancing across its sleek skin.'

A mythical selkie (which we will look at later in this chapter) has answered a wish made at its gravestone. The story was inspired by the real-life legend of a selkie's grave within the grounds of St Trothan's Church in Castletown, near to where I grew up in the Scottish Highlands.

NUGGLE

(Also known as: *njuggle, neugle, shoepultie* or *shoopiltee*)

A nuggle is another of the legendary water horses from Scottish folklore. The creature generally walks the shores and frequents the lochs, streams and rivers of the Shetland Islands. Nuggles are always male and only emerge at night to play pranks on the island's residents and those travelling through its territory.

The nuggle has a very distinctive wheel-like tail and, unlike its bloodthirsty counterparts that we've met up to this point, the mythical monster isn't considered to be evil and murderous, preferring mischievous chaos over outright malevolent deeds.

The *Dictionary of the Scots Language* states that like so many other mythical creatures from the Scottish Highlands and Islands, the nuggle (neugle, nigle, nogle, nyogle, nygul and the many other spelling variations) gets its name from an Old Norse word, nykr, and may have similar origins to the Middle Low German or the Middle Dutch water demon, necker.

In *An Etymological Glossary of the Shetland & Orkney Dialect*, Thomas Edmondston states that the term 'niogle' is of Gothic origins, stemming from the word gner (meaning horse) and el (meaning water). There are many commonalities and influences from across the world that have resulted in the modern water horse legend known as the nuggle.

In *Trolls, Hillfolk, Finns and Picts*, Alan Bruford states that the nuggle was able to shape-shift, but generally maintained its water horse form and never transformed into a human. The creature's coat resembled those of the water, ranging from a deep blue-grey of the depths to the white-grey of the waves.

In *Scottish, Shetlandic and Germanic Water Tales*, folklorist Karl Blind states that the nuggle was native only to Shetland, though similar tales of the creature have been found in the Orkney Islands.

In *The Folklore of Orkney and Shetland*, Ernest W. Marwick states that you could identify the nuggle by its unique wheel-like tail. Karl Blind adds that the creature rarely attacked humans and even the pranks it played were never too dangerous in nature.

In *Shetland Folk-Lore*, John Spence says that only the mysterious Finns were able to mount and ride a nuggle. The Finns were a magical race of evil sorcerers from Viking legends (not real-life Finnish people) who researchers believe likely originated from myths surrounding people from Lapland (see *Finfolk* earlier in this chapter).

Older research suggests that, if a nuggle is able to trick a human into mounting him, he would then drag the poor victim to the deepest part of the lake. However, the majority of nuggle legends contradict this behaviour, pointing to the generally kinder disposition of the mythical water horse. Perhaps on some occasions, the nuggle legends have been mistaken for the myths around their more malevolent cousins, the kelpies.

The *Orkneyjar* website describes one of these older tales, which takes place on the Orkney island of Hoy. The many pools and streams of the island seemingly contained many malevolent versions of the nuggle, particularly around the Water o' Hoy, the Little Loch at Rackwick and the Pegal Burn.

At the Pegal Burn, it's said that the nuggle would hide on the island of Rysa Little, which gave it a perfect view of approaching victims coming to cross the bridge over the burn. The nuggle would then trick or attack the unsuspecting passerby, dragging them into the water.

According to the folklore of Shetland, a group of islanders once captured a nuggle and chained it to a standing stone that was situated between two lochs. However, the mythical beast was so strong that it escaped. The marks in the stone from where it fought against its chain were the only evidence the men had of their successful capture.

Folklorist Jessie M. Saxby provides reasoning for so many legends surrounding the creature, stating that it was once used as a warning to keep children from venturing into deep water or playing inside dangerous watermills.

Parents would often add the embellishment to the legend that, should children remain at a safe distance from the water, a nuggle may appear and play them a pleasant tune.

John Spence, who actually lived in Lerwick, confirms that the myths and legends around the nuggle were told as precautionary tales that handed down life lessons to the younger generations, usually by grandparents.

OILLIPHÉIST

(Irish: *ollphéist*)

The Oilliphéist is actually an Irish legend but is included in this collection because stories of this creature were believed to have inspired the origins of the Loch Ness Monster.

The Oilliphéist name comes from the Irish oll (meaning great) and péist (meaning worm, fabulous beast, monster or reptile). This provides a great description of the mythical monster, which is said to be a huge sea-serpent that inhabits the rivers and lakes of Ireland.

Many Irish legends contain heroes and saints battling the great serpent. In his *Dictionary of Celtic Mythology*, Peter Berresford Ellis tells the story of Saint Patrick (the patron saint of Ireland) who arrived in the land to drive the snakes and serpents off the island, including the Oilliphéist, who cut the route of the River Shannon upon hearing of the saint's arrival. In the legendary folktale, a piper named Ó Ruairc (O'Rourke) was said to have got really drunk and was swallowed whole by the Oilliphéist. Either too drunk to notice or care, the piper continued playing his music while inside the Oilliphéist's stomach.

The mythical monster grew so annoyed with the piper's endless tunes, that it spat him back out. In *Monsters of Film, Fiction and Fable: The cultural links between the human and inhuman*, Chris Cairney states that this legend (alongside one around the Caoránach) was the inspiration for the Loch Ness Monster tales.

The other influence, the Caoránach (sometimes Coal), was also an Oilliphéist and believed to be the mother of demons. Saint Patrick was said to have banished the beast to Loch Dearg in Donegal, possibly later influencing the serpent in the loch myths from which Nessie was born.

The full legend around this goes that Fionn mac Cumhaill and the Fianna were on a quest to slay a hag in the Lough Dearg area and managed to kill her from a great distance with an arrow. When they reached the body, another member of their party warned them not to break the hag's thigh bone, or it would release a terrible monster.

Unfortunately, one member of the team named Conan decided to do just that. A small hairy worm fell from the bone and quickly grew in size to become the fearsome Caoránach. Unleashed with a great hunger, the monster began to relentlessly devour cattle, until Conan made amends by entering the beast's open mouth and slaying it with a sword. Folklorists say that Loch Dearg is named after the blood that spilt from the Caoránach, as it dyed the rocks red.

In an alternative ending, it's Saint Patrick himself who slays the monster (though in some tales he fails to fully defeat the creature and banishes it to the loch).

In one final tale, told by Gary Branigan in *Cavan Folk Tales*, there was once a girl called Sionnan who angered the Salmon of Knowledge by throwing rocks at him. To stop the girl the salmon summoned an Oilliphéist and ordered it to attack the annoying girl. The Oilliphéist did as it was commanded and killed the girl.

SEA MITHER

(Also known as: *Mither o' the Sea*)

The Sea Mither is a powerful Orcadian summer spirit that fights an eternal struggle for control of the seas against her arch-nemesis, Teran, an equally powerful winter spirit.

Folklorist Walter Traill Dennison, an Orkney resident, states that during the summer months, the Sea Mither is at the height of her powers and is able to defeat Teran, imprison him and calm the choppy waters. At the same time, she manages to prevent the demonic nuckelavee from attacking the land.

Her benevolent powers were said to warm the waters, calm the breeze and enable sea creatures to reproduce. Gradually though, the Sea Mither tires and as the year wears on Teran is able to wrestle control of the seas from her once more. And the dreaded nuckelavee is unleashed once more.

The term Mither is a Scots variant of 'mother', which was (and still is) used frequently in my hometown of Wick, in Caithness. The name Teran is believed to have originated from Orcadian dialect meaning 'furious anger' or from the Norse word 'tyrren', which means angry, like the seas are in winter.

Twice a year, as either the powers of the Sea Mither or Teran grow or wane, the two battle for control of the seas, which causes gale force winds and huge waves. The howl of the coming winter winds is said to be the anguished cries of Teran as he fights his way out of his imprisonment.

Dennison tells how the Sea Mither is forced to retire and rest during the winter so that she can come back in the spring to battle again. Nobody quite knows where she goes during this time, but they are confident she will always return. Her return was known as the beginning of the 'Vore Tullye' (Spring Struggle). In the autumn, when Teran breaks free, another battle is fought, known as the 'Gore Vellye' (Autumn Tumult).

Folklorist Ernest Marwick states that the Sea Mither and Teran are the personifications of the natural changes that take place each autumn and spring, as weather patterns improve or deteriorate as we move into either summer or winter.

Dennison explains that this was a common element of legends from many cultures, who struggled to explain natural phenomena, without the aid of modern scientific knowledge.

Nevertheless, fishermen of the Shetland Islands used to (and may still) whisper a silent petition to the Sea Mither to offer them protection from wild waters and a bountiful catch.

As the old Orcadian verse goes:

Bit luck thee niver noo in Vore,Cin man hear tale o' Teran
Rampagan' on da ocean floor, Fur folk ir little carin
Hoo tullyas or brullyas. Fowt wi' de great Sea-mither
'swordship gae lordship, Tae ane or else the tither.

SELKIE

(Also known as: *selky, seilkie, sejlki, silkie, silkey, saelkie, sylkie, selchie, selkie fowk* or *seal folk*)

Selkies are one of the most popular creatures from Celtic and Norse legends, with their myths and folktales particularly prevalent in the north of Scotland. Selkies are capable of therianthropy, which is the ability to shape-shift into the form of an animal, in this case a seal, by shedding their skin.

Selkie is the Scots language word for a mythical creature that has many variations in spelling (see above) but is listed in the Scottish National Dictionary as being diminutive for the word 'selch' which means 'grey seal'.

In *The Grey Selkie*, Alan Bruford argues that the term selkie is simply a name for the grey seal (Halichoerus grypus) and that any seal can be a selkie, whether it has the ability to transform into human form or not. However, the legends have collectively borrowed this name to describe the shape-shifting creature.

In *Orkney Folk-Lore and Sea Legends*, Walter Traill Dennison states that the term selkie is reserved for any seal larger than a normal grey seal, thus possibly identifying the animal as one of the shape-shifting selkie folk.

The majority of selkie legends revolve around female selkies, who are often forced into marrying a human after having their seal-skin stolen while naked on the beach.

In the traditional 'Selkie-Wife' legend, the husband locks the seal-skin inside a chest and hides the key. However, one day the husband returns home to discover the chest has been opened and his wife's clothes are scattered across the floor, as she has returned to the sea.

Dennison recalls another similar tale, where the selkie-wife regains her skin with help from her daughter, who had once spotted it being hidden under the roof.

In many other versions of this legend, the selkie-wife spends her days longing to return to her home beneath the waves. Even if she has children with her human husband, she still escapes to the sea as soon as she discovers where her seal-skin is hidden. Often, she is going home to reunite with her selkie husband whom she married before she was captured. In the traditional versions of the tale, she is never seen again. But to lighten the legend slightly for younger age groups, children's versions of the tale may have the selkie visit them again in either human or seal form.

In *Supernatural Beings in the Far North: Folklore, Folk Belief, and the Selkie*, Nancy Cassell McEntire discusses the hereditary traits of children born from the mixed marriages of selkies and humans. Often, children with a selkie mother will have webbed hands, but children with a selkie father may also have toes made from a horn-like material that requires regular filing or clipping away.

In a twist on the traditional tale, some legends have the selkies making humans fall in love with them and luring their new partners into the water, after which they never return to the land.

Perhaps these lovesick humans were whisked away to an underwater selkie home, where some legends say that the selkies would shed their seal-skin and walk around as humans, breathing air. Geologist and antiquarian, Samuel Hibbert, suggests that their skins may have simply been a 'sea-dress' which they wore to travel between their underwater home and the land, but that every skin was unique to that selkie and irreplaceable.

Dennison states that the more elusive male selkies are very handsome and often seek out human women who are dissatisfied with their current lives, such as the bored wives of fishermen who spend too much time at sea.

In *A Description of the Shetland Islands*, Hibbert tells a selkie legend called *Gioga's Son*. In this tale, a pod of seals are resting in the Ve Skerries, a group of rocky islands three miles northwest of Papa Stour in Shetland. Unfortunately, a group of local fishermen from Papa Stour ambushed the seals, skinned them and left with their skins.

Unknown to the fishermen, these seals were actually selkies. Once their blood hit the water, the sea began to surge and threatened to sink their boat. In their haste to escape, a solitary fisherman was left behind on the rocky islands.

The fisherman watched in amazement as another group of selkies emerged from the water, shed their skins and tended to their wounded companions. The ambushed selkies healed in their human form, though they mourned the loss of their skins, without which they couldn't return to their home beneath the waves.

One male selkie, Ollavitinus, was particularly distressed because he could no longer return to his wife. However, his mother, Gioga, noticed the lone fisherman and decided to strike a bargain with him. She would swim him safely back to Papa Stour, in return for the stolen skins. Once back on land, the fisherman honoured the bargain and gave the selkies their skins back.

The fishermen in this legend didn't realise that the seals they were attacking were selkies and it was rare for residents of Orkney and Shetland to harm seals in general, for it supposedly brought bad luck. It was only during the hardest of times that locals would harvest the skin and blubber of seals, lest they fall foul of the selkie's revenge.

Folklorist Ernest Marwick tells the tale of a group of Orcadian crofters who had gathered their sheep to graze on a group of small islands. One summer evening, while on his way home, one of the crofters killed a seal. That night, all of his sheep that he had left on the islands mysteriously disappeared. All the sheep belonging to the other crofters, who did not kill a seal, were still safely grazing on their islands.

Dennison states that some of the more obscure legends suggest that selkies are either fallen angels or humans who had committed a sin, thereby condemning their soul and only allowing them to change into human form once every seven years. Author, Lowry Charles Wimberly, noted that the number seven appears quite often in balladry, including in a popular traditional folk song of the Orkney and Shetland Islands.

The Great Silkie of Sule Skerry (also known as *The Grey Selkie of Sule Skerry*) is a ballad that contains details about the shape-shifting nature of the selkies. In the song, a woman's son is taken by his father, the great selkie of Sule Skerry, who can transform at will between seal and human form. The woman later marries a gunner who harpoons both the selkie and her son. Part of the melancholy ballad goes:

'I am a man upon the land
I am a silkie in the sea
And when I'm far frae every strand
My dwelling is in Sule Skerry

Alas, alas, this woefu' fate
This weary fate that's been laid on me
That a man should have come frae the wast' o' Hoy
Tae the Norowa' lands t'hae a bairn wi' me

My dear, I'll wed ye wi' a ring
Wi' a ring, my dear, I'll wed wi' thee
Thou may go wed wi' whom thou will
I'm sure you'll never wed wi' me

Thou will nurse my bonnie son
For seeven lang years upon your knee
An' at the end o' seeven lang years
I'll come and pay thy nurse's fee'

Like many legends, the origins of selkie myths and folktales may actually be based on real-life events that took place at a time when we understood less about the world.

Cassandra Eason pointed out that many physiological conditions and abnormalities were untreatable in the past, including webbed fingers and toes, which may have led to people being considered children of mythical creatures.

In *The Origin of the Selkie-folk: Documented Finmen Sightings* on the Orkneyjar website, Sigurd Towrie writes that children with scaly skin were often believed to be descended from selkies, but were likely suffering from a genetic skin disorder, such as ichthyosis. He also suggests that children born with the head of a seal may actually have been suffering from the rare birth defect anencephaly, where children are born without parts of their brain or skull.

Many non-medical explanations for the origins of selkies have also been proposed; with folklorist David MacRitchie suggesting that Finnish and Sami women may have been described as selkies due to their seal-skin clothing and boats. The removal of these skin-like items of clothing to dry them out on the shore was likely misinterpreted by those watching from afar.

The selkie legends have inspired many creative people. Scottish poet George Mackay Brown penned the story *Sealskin*, Eric Linklater wrote *Sealskin Trousers*, Robin Robertson wrote the poem *At Roane Head* and Michael Corrigan created the novel *Brewer's Odyssey*.

As mentioned on the nuckelavee page, my own collection of Scottish stories, *Mysteries and Misadventures: Tales from the Highlands*, contains a benevolent selkie that comes to the aid of a woman in distress.

SEONAIDH

(Also known as: *Seonadh*. Anglicised: *Shony* or *Shoney*)

Scottish writer Martin Martin, author of *A Description of the Western Islands of Scotland*, says that the Seonaidh is a water spirit who inhabits the Isle of Lewis, the largest island in the Outer Hebrides. Edward Dwelly's *Scottish Gaelic Dictionary* lists seonadh, without the 'i', as meaning either Druidism, sorcery or augury. Seonaidh is also a pet form of the English and Hebrew name John.

Martin tells the legend of the magical water spirit Seonaidh, stating that residents of the Isle of Lewis would try to appease the spirit with a cup of ale. To do this, the men would gather at the church of St. Mulway (Maelrubha) with their offering of a bag of malt. Once there, all the malt was brewed together into ale. One person would then wade waist-deep into the sea at night with a cup of this ale and say the following:

'Seonaidh, I give thee this cup of ale, hoping that thou wilt be so good as to send us plenty of seaware (seaweed used as a fertilizer) for enriching our ground during the coming year.'

The chosen person would then throw the ale into the sea. Everybody would then gather back in the church and light a candle on the altar. The next night, they would drink the rest of the ale. This suggests Seonaidh was originally a god, whose worship had become ritualised. It may also be possible that given Seonaidh is the Scottish Gaelic form of John, that they are worshipping one of the Saints John.

SHELLYCOAT

The shellycoat is a mythical bogeyman who lives in the rivers and streams of Scotland and the north of England. The creature gets its name from the coat of shells it is said to wear. You can tell when a shellycoat is near because you can hear its coat rattling when it walks.

Katharine Briggs believes the shellycoats are mischievous, rather than malicious, and are known to play pranks on travellers who have trespassed into their territory. An example would be for the shellycoat to call for help, as if they were drowning, then laugh as the trespasser attempts to find where the call came from.

In *Deutsche Mythologie*, Jacob Grimm states that the shellycoat is a type of Scottish goblin (rather than water spirit) and claims it is actually the same creature as the German Schellenrock, which wears a bellcoat. Grimm tells of a domesticated version of the shellycoat:

'A pück (home-sprite) served the monks of a Mecklenburg monastery for thirty years, in kitchen, stall and elsewhere; he was thoroughly good-natured, and only bargained for 'tunicam de diversis coloribus, et tintinnabulis plenam' (a parti-coloured coat with tinkling bells). In Scotland there lived a goblin Shellycoat, and we saw that the dwarfs of the Mid. Ages also loved bells. The bells on the dress of a fool still attest his affinity to the shrewd and merry goblin.'

Most researchers agree that this domesticated household version of the shellycoat is very much in contrast to the wild Scottish water spirit described in most legends.

STOOR WORM

The Stoor Worm is an enormous sea serpent from the Orkney Islands, with putrid breath that would contaminate crops, kill animals and harm humans. The legend of the Stoor Worm (also known as Mester Stoor Worm) is believed to have originated from Norse Mythology, where Jörmungandr (meaning 'huge monster') is the Midgard (World) Serpent.

According to Norse legends, Odin (the god of wisdom, poetry, death, divination, and magic) cast Jörmungandr into the ocean, where he grew so large that he encircled the world and grasped his own tail. Ragnarök (Old Norse for Doom of the Gods, the Scandinavian end of the world) was said to begin when he finally releases his tail, which would cause a great battle, the death of many heroic figures, natural disasters and the submersion of the world in water.

Legends state that each Saturday, at sunrise, the Stoor Worm would wake from its slumber, open its mouth and yawn nine times. A king, learning that the beast was approaching his land, was advised by a sorcerer that the beast must be fed a meal of seven virgins to appease his appetite. So the king followed the wise man's advice and every Saturday he sacrificed seven virgins to the beast by tying them up and abandoning them on the shore, ready for the serpent to sweep them into its mouth. However, this practice soon earned the ire of the island residents, who were concerned that they would soon run out of sacrificial virgins.

The king once again turned to the wise man for advice and was told that he must sacrifice his own daughter, Princess Gem-de-lovely. The king was distraught by this advice and was desperate for another solution, so he offered his daughter's hand in marriage (and the magical sword Sickersnapper, inherited from Odin) to anyone who could rid the world of the monster.

On hearing the king's offer, many heroes came forward. However, when standing on the beach and looking out to sea at the task they faced, none of them were brave enough to fight the beast.

Assipattle, the seventh son of a good-hearted local farmer, heard the king's offer and planned to defeat the beast. However, he was known as a lazy daydreamer who would often spin tales of himself fighting imaginary foes, and so was roundly ridiculed by his friends and family when he announced his plan.

Meanwhile, to save his daughter, the desperate king made plans to fight the Stoor Worm himself using Sickersnapper. He had his guards ready his boat at the water's edge and was due to set sail in the morning.

Undeterred by the mocking laughter of his loved ones, Assipattle stole his father's horse during the night and set off in search of the creature, arriving just as the great serpent opened its mouth at sunrise. The resourceful Assipattle spotted his opportunity, stole some hot peat from an elderly woman's cottage and tricked the king's guard into giving him the very boat that was meant to carry the king to battle the beast.

During one great yawn, Assipattle sailed the boat down into the creature's stomach. There he plunged the burning peat into the liver of the great beast, starting a blaze and causing the Stoor Worm to retch, which carried his boat back out of the monster's mouth to the safety of the crowded beach.

The islanders watched the Stoor Worm's death throes from the safety of a nearby hillside, out of reach of the great waves, earthquakes and plumes of black smoke emanating from the creature. As it died, its teeth fell out and became the islands of Orkney, Shetland and the Faroes. Its body became Iceland and its tongue created the Baltic Sea.

The king kept his word and awarded Assipattle both the magic sword and Princess Gem-de-lovely's hand in marriage. It's said that the celebrations lasted for nine weeks and they lived happily ever after. A lesson, then, to never give up on your daydreams, no matter how wild they may seem to those around you.

Ernest W. Marwick states that there is a natural aspect behind the origins of the Stoor Worm legend. In Shetland, residents believed that a great creature lived far out at sea, who was so large that it would take it six hours to inhale a breath, and another six hours to exhale. Marwick noted that this was likely a pre-science explanation of the cycle of the tides.

E. S. Hartland states that these types of stories represented a cultural shift away from the primitive, suppressive nature of having to sacrifice people to great beasts, as humanity became more enlightened.

TANGIE

(Also known as: *tongie*)

A tangie is another shape-shifting water spirit from the Orkney and Shetland Islands, which regularly takes the form of either a horse or a man.

Katharine Briggs states that its name comes from its appearance, as the creature was often reported as being covered in seaweed from the genus Fucus, also known as tang. A malevolent spirit, the tangie gained notoriety for its attacks on lone travellers. It particularly enjoyed abducting young women from the roads and pathways near the lochs. Once captured, the victims would be dragged beneath the surface of the water and eaten alive.

In *Water-Beings in Shetlandic Folk-Lore*, J. A. Teit claims that the tangie is able to cause 'derangement' in both animals and humans, making them easier to capture.

In *Scottish Folklore*, Raymond Lamont-Brown tells the most famous tangie legend. There was once a man from Shetland called Black Eric, who had chosen to be a sheep rustler. He had somehow partnered with a tangie and rode it when committing his crimes, with the creature's magic assisting in their evil deeds.

One day, Black Eric was killed by a crofter called Sandy Breamer, his body falling into the sea. Locals thought this would bring the reign of terror to an end. However, the tangie continued raiding the local crofts and scaring young women, having learnt from his fallen partner-in-crime.

WATER BULL

(Scottish Gaelic: *tarbh uisge*)

The water bull is a mythical monster similar to the legendary Scottish water horses, but which prefers the form of a bull. The shape-shifting beast is said to haunt many moorland lochs and occasionally takes human form.

Edward Dwelly states that the Scottish Gaelic tar tarbh-uisge (or tarbh uisge) translates as 'water bull, sea bull or cow' of a fabulous nature, suggesting a mythical monster, above and beyond your average water-dwelling bovine.

In *Popular Tales of the West Highlands*, John Francis Campbell notes that the water bull is able to live on the land as a human. Folklorists agree that, in the water bull legends, the creature is much more amiable than its equine counterparts, but can become a powerful and violent black beast when angered.

The majority of legends refer to the male of the species. However, Sir Walter Scott tells the story of a water cow, when residents attempted to drain Loch na Beiste in search of the mythical creature living there. A water cow was also believed to live in a small loch near Borrodale, on the Isle of Skye.

In *The Lore of Scotland: A Guide to Scottish Legends*, Jennifer Westwood and Sophia Kingshill discuss the offspring of water bulls mating with regular cows. They note that water cows spotted near Leverburgh, on the Isle of Harris, produced calves with purple-coloured ears.

Folklorist John Gregorson Campbell states that the offspring of water bulls are 'knife-eared'. He explains that this is due to the water bulls not having any ears, so calves are born with smaller half-ears.

Campbell also tells the legend of a water bull who lived on Islay, in the Inner Hebrides. This tale is very similar to a previous story about the water horse each-uisge, but contains more detail and a different twist at the end.

One day a calf was born to a normal cow and an old lady (who was later discovered to be a witch) advised the herdsman to separate it from the rest of the herd.

The witch had noticed something special about the calf – it had been born with an ear deformity that identified it as potentially being a water bull. With this in mind, she ordered the herdsman to rear the calf on milk from three different cows and isolate it within its own stable for at least seven years.

Several years later, a young woman was grazing cattle at a nearby loch, when she met a handsome man. The pair quickly became close and following a lengthy conversation, they decided to rest on the grass. The man lay his head on her lap and fell asleep.

This was the moment the girl first noticed something odd about the stranger. The man's hair was entwined with seaweed, so the girl assumed he must be one of the mythical water horses disguised in human form.

The girl stood up and tried to run back to the safety of her farm, but the man woke up. Seeing the girl running away, the man transformed into a horse and chased after her.

As the girl approached the farm, the witch heard her cries for help and ordered the herdsman to release the water bull from its stable. The mythical bull charged at the legendary horse and the two creatures entered into a great battle which raged across the land until they both fell into the sea. The water horse was never seen again, but the remains of the bull were discovered the next day. He had died protecting the humans that raised him.

The kind nature of the water bull may be the reason why there are so few legends about capturing or killing this mythical creature. Scottish geologist, John MacCulloch, does tell a tale though of locals who attempted to catch a water bull that frequented the area between Loch Awe and Loch Rannoch.

The hunters set a trap for the beast by tying a sheep to an oak tree, but the shackle they used to catch the water bull was not strong enough and it broke free. Another legend tells the story of a farmer and his two sons who were said to hunt the water bull with a musket filled with silver sixpence coins. But they failed, as so many others had before them, to capture a live water bull.

The witch in the previous legend who noticed that the calf was different from the others was actually an exception to the normal beliefs of the time, as James MacKillop states it was well-known that you should kill a water bull calf at birth before it can bring disaster to the rest of the herd.

This belief may have stemmed from warnings for farmers to be on the lookout for deformities within their herd, which they would not want to be bred into future generations, for fear of devaluing their cattle and thereby jeopardising their livelihoods. This was particularly true at a time of heightened superstitious beliefs.

In *Scottish Folklore*, Raymond Lamont-Brown notes that it's not so easy to kill a water bull calf, as they are immune to the traditional method of drowning them, so other ways must be found.

However, Jennifer Westwood and Sophia Kingshill refer to a collection of stories published by George Sutherland which seem to suggest that in the Highlands the hybrid offspring of water bulls and normal cows were actually considered to be a higher quality of cattle. This demonstrates the regional variations in the legends of the water bull.

If we look at the origins of these tales, from various parts of Scotland, we can see that bulls, in general, have always held a spiritual place in a number of Celtic beliefs. In *Animals in Celtic Life and Myth*, Miranda Green states that the animal was so revered as a symbol of abundance and fertility within certain Celtic cults that one of those tribes, the Taurini, even adopted the bull's name.

Fittingly, this makes the water bull a powerful animal, an intriguing legend and a historic symbol of our ancestors with which to end our exploration of Scotland's greatest mythical monsters.

AUTHOR'S NOTES

Having sailed on a boat cruise down Loch Ness, I can see why the huge and beautiful body of water has achieved its legendary status. Even on a calm day, the odd-looking wave or shadow on the water draws your eye away from the stunning scenery.

And just for a moment, you think you might be, after all this time, the one to finally capture Nessie grinning away as it ends the longest ever game of hide-and-seek by popping its head out the water. Alas, all your dreams of monster stardom are dashed when the boat draws closer at an agonisingly slow speed and you realise you have been filming a floating log for the past ten minutes.

Growing up in Wick, in the Highlands, I was aware of local legends, like the selkie's grave in Castletown, from a very young age. As kids, we were surrounded by forests, mountains and the sea, which to our young imaginations contained all manner of beasts.

We built our huts and bases at 'banshee forest' from random items our resourceful younger selves acquired, but we never went up there at night.

My over-active imagination would cause me to suddenly swim a little bit faster every time I dived into the Trinkie, an outdoor swimming pool cut into the cliffs and filled by the North Sea, as I felt (what I hope was) a stray bit of seaweed brush against my leg.

We travelled to Orkney on both school and family trips, immersing ourselves in the history and legends of its islands. One of my favourite memories is of another school trip, to Dunrobin Castle in Sutherland, where my younger self was in awe of the skulls, stuffed heads and life-size replicas of various animals that adorned the hunting trophies room.

These memories and my growing interest in the cultural history and folklore tales of Scotland inspired this book.

Thanks go, as always, to my amazing team of proofreaders, who catch the too-excited-to-stop-typing parts of my early drafts and help me shape my writing and ideas into a book that everyone can enjoy.

If you haven't already done so, check out my other Scottish short story collections. And thank you for reading!

Aaron Mullins

ABOUT THE AUTHOR

Aaron Mullins

Dr Aaron Mullins is an award-winning, internationally published psychologist. He's also an Amazon bestselling author and is known for exploring powerful psychological experiences in his books.

Aaron has a wealth of experience in the publishing industry, with expertise in supporting fellow authors achieve their writing goals. He started Birdtree Books Publishing where he worked as Editor-in-Chief. He also partnered with World Reader Charity, getting ebooks into Africa and sponsoring English lessons in an under-tree school in India.

Aaron taught Academic Writing at Coventry University and has achieved great success with his bestselling short story anthologies. Aaron's book *How to Write Fiction: A Creative Writing Guide for Authors* has become a staple reference book for writers and those interested in a publishing career.

Aaron's website, www.AaronMullins.com contains free resources to support authors with inspiration and practical help, with many writing, publishing and marketing guides.

Originally from the Scottish Highlands, Aaron spent many years south of the border but now lives by the beach on the west coast of Scotland, where he devotes most of his non-writing time to charity work, raising his daughter and travelling to beautiful places.

AVAILABLE FROM AMAZON

Mullins Collection of Best New Fiction

Explore worlds populated with strange creatures. Ghouls that feed in the darkness of the London underground in *The Orphaned City* and the strange patient who stalks the halls of a mental asylum in *Inferiority Complex*. Discover worlds where humans are the most curious of all, the charming smile of the mysterious Jack in *Knowing Jack* and the devious mind of Red in *The Path I Set Upon*.

Perhaps the next story will spark into life a new idea, the kind that Jake develops from an overheard conversation in *Dreamworld*. Or question our very existence, like the revelations of Professor Westerham in *Reflection*. It might even lead to a dangerous hunt for untold riches, which Ryan experiences in *The Hassam Legacy*.

You may discover a love for stories you wouldn't have considered before. Fiction does that to you. It draws you into its welcoming embrace. Sometimes the welcome is warm, like the strength of Helen after dealing with death in *Coming of Age*. Other times you feel an icy chill as the story grips you, like the terror that claws at Meg when she hears her parrot speak in *Scared to Death*.

Nine different worlds are waiting to be explored. Each hides a secret, a twist that awaits discovery by an adventurous reader. Welcome to our worlds.

AVAILABLE FROM AMAZON

Mullins Collection of Best New Horror

Horror. The stories that keep you awake at night. The tales that have you checking underneath the bed... or wondering whether that really is just a shadow in the corner.

In this collection, you will find early stories from four horror writers, all guaranteed to instil a feeling of dread deep within your bones as your shaking fingers struggle to turn the page.

A dark secret is revealed in *My Natalie*, a tale of vengeful love. A home with a hidden past threatens to destroy a young family in *The House*.

The restless spirit of a young girl has to deliver an important message in *Phantom Memory*. Finally, thrill-seeking Melanie gets more than she bargained for, as she explores the mysterious festival in *The Secrets of Hidden Places*.

The horror awaits...

AVAILABLE FROM AMAZON

Mysteries and Misadventures:
Tales from the Highlands

Ten tales set in the Highlands of Scotland.
True childhood secrets revealed in the Story Behind the
Stories.

In *The Road Trip,* a couple make a surprise stop at a
guesthouse with a deadly history, looking for its next
victims. In *Secrets of the River,* an unopened box is
dragged from the river. A hastily scrawled message from
the past, stolen by a young woman who is now being
hunted. With time running out, can she survive its secrets?

In *Equal To and Greater Than,* James has a 1 in 54
condition. Attacked and humiliated, he must harness the
power of his gifts and become the hero he needs to be. In
The Gala Queen, it's Halloween night. A prank goes
wrong. A young girl dies and the boy responsible has got
away with it. Until the annual town gala, when the gala
queen comes seeking vengeance.

In *Revenge of the Green Man,* Charlie plots to get his
stolen CD back, dragging his friend into ever-crazier
schemes. In *The House on Lovers' Lane,* a boy is missing
and two girls lie to their parents so they can spend the
night drinking in a field. But when a dare goes wrong they
soon discover the danger they are in.

In *Call of the Nuckelavee,* a woman stalks the sandy
dunes, following the voice of her drowned father. In the

turbulent sea, she comes face to face with a creature that has haunted her nightmares. In *Black Dog in the Devil's Bothy*, a troubled woman hikes through a storm. She strays from the mountain path and loses her way in the forest. Taking shelter in a bothy, she discovers her fears have followed her to the darkest of places.

In *Last Train South*, a woman boards a train with a heavy suitcase. Evidence she must dispose of, with the help of her friends. In *Stolen Peace*, a nuclear biologist just wants to spend his final days camping in the woods and reading his book. Unfortunately, trained killers want him to return the item he stole.

AVAILABLE FROM AMAZON

Scottish Killers: 25 True Crime Stories

25 True Crime Stories of Murder and Malice

A fascinating collection of Scotland's most deadly serial killers and notorious murderers.

A chilling anthology of the true crime stories that shocked the world.

The details of each case are revealed.
The motives of each killer are explored.

Each murder is examined in a new light, stripped of the sensationalism of newspapers, and with the greatest amount of compassion and respect paid to the victims and their families.

This book analyses the minds of those who would commit such horrific crimes.

What drove Ian Brady to kill?
Which serial killer got away with 14 further suspected murders?
Which gangland killer became a successful Scottish artist?

Discover the answers to these questions in this book, where more difficult and devastating truths are also revealed.

AVAILABLE FROM AMAZON

Scottish Urban Legends:
50 Myths and True Stories

A HUGE collection of Scottish Urban Legends, Myths and True Stories. The definitive guide to the legendary stories that reveal Scotland's mysterious past.

Each tale is dazzlingly retold for a modern audience. Gather around the fireside and hear stories from a land filled with magic and mystery. Feel the rich history brought to life through folktales passed down through generations. Hear the true stories that lurk amongst these myths, things that the author has witnessed with his own eyes, revealed for the very first time.

Where is the most haunted road in Scotland? Who got caught cheating while playing cards with the devil? Which military camouflage suit got its name from a forest faerie? What ancient rhyme can summon a violent poltergeist?

Roadside phantoms, cunning spirits and real-world killers, this enchanting collection has them all. From tales of great battles to pagan rituals that are still performed today. Discover the locations where you can see and feel these experiences for yourself, if you dare.

Huddle closer to the fire, read the book and decide for yourself which of the legends are true.

THANK YOU

Thank you for reading my book! I always devote a lot of time to making my books as enjoyable as possible for you.

I have a day job working for a lovely charity, so I write on my days off and in the evenings once my daughter has gone to bed and my family duties are done for the day.

So if you enjoyed reading my book, please kindly take a minute to leave a nice review so others can discover me and my writing.

I really appreciate you supporting me as an author and it inspires me to write more books for you!

Amazon: amazon.com/author/aaronmullins

FOLLOW ME

Twitter: twitter.com/DrAaronMullins
Facebook: facebook.com/aaronmullinsauthor
Instagram: instagram.com/draaronmullins
Youtube: youtube.com/c/AaronMullins
Pinterest: pinterest.com/aaronmullinsauthor

HEAR IT FIRST

Head to my website and click the 'Follow' button to be notified when I publish a new blog post, or a new book!

www.aaronmullins.com

Printed in Great Britain
by Amazon

77881769R00103